Books by Barbara Morgenroth

RIDE A PROUD HORSE

LAST JUNIOR YEAR

TRAMPS LIKE US

IMPOSSIBLE CHARLIE

Impossible
Charlie

Impossible
Charlie

by BARBARA MORGENROTH

illustrated by VELMA ILSLEY

Atheneum   1979   New York

To My Mother

Morgenroth, Barbara.
Impossible Charlie.
SUMMARY: A horse that seemed ideal when Jackie got him
turns out to have too much of a mind of his own.
[1. Horses–Fiction] I. Ilsley, Velma. II. Title.
PZ7.M82669Im   [Fic]   79-10447
ISBN 0-689-30718-7
Text copyright © 1979 by Barbara Morgenroth
Illustrations copyright © 1979 by Velma Ilsley
All rights reserved
Composed by American–Stratford Graphic Services, Inc.,
Brattleboro, Vermont
Printed and bound by R. R. Donnelley & Sons,
Crawfordsville, Indiana
Design by Marjorie Zaum
First Edition

Impossible
Charlie

Chapter
One

JACKIE DRAGGED HER FOOT ALONG THE ROAD AS SHE
came down the hill on her bicycle because the hand
brakes didn't work. Hadn't worked for months. She
was going faster than she would have liked, but still
not fast enough to get home in time. Reaching the
bottom of the hill, she stood on the pedals and raced
towards home. At top speed the whole trip, she would
be only a little late and her mother might not notice,
but there was still the hill before her, which seemed
about as tall as Mount Washington in New Hamp-
shire.

By the time she had made it to her driveway, she
was out of breath and practically dropped the bike
trying to jump off. She made two swipes with her

foot at the kickstand, but when it didn't come down, she settled for leaning the bike up against the garage wall and ran into the house.

"You're late." Her mother was at the stove, scooping mashed potatoes from a pot to a serving bowl.

Jackie glanced at the wall clock. Twenty after six. She was twenty minutes late. "I'm sorry."

"Do you have a believable excuse?"

"I think it's a good one."

"Let me hear it, I could use a laugh. It's been a dull day so far."

Jackie was relieved that her mother wasn't going to lecture or scold. "I finished riding Moose in plenty of time. I got him all cleaned up and had him standing in the hall ready to feed him, when I remembered I had to put oil on his hooves today. The blacksmith said every other day last time he was there."

"This sounds like a long story. Why don't you set the table while you go on."

Jackie grabbed the napkins and silverware from the drawer and went into the dining room. "So I ran into the tack room and I couldn't find the oil where I left it last time. Lisa is such a slob, she can't put anything back where it belongs. So it took me a while to find the can, which she had left hidden on the floor by the feed bin. Then I had to find the hoofpick, which wasn't hung on the hook but was in the brush box. I looked at the clock, and it said five thirty, and I knew if I didn't leave soon, I was going to be late. I didn't have any trouble doing Moose's front feet, but when I got to the back ones, I couldn't get his foot off the floor. I pulled and shoved, and he had his weight square on both."

"Why didn't Lisa help you?" Mrs. Knapp called from the kitchen.

"This is her day for piano lessons. I was all alone. So after about fifteen minutes. I pried his foot up enough so I could just get the hoof pick underneath. He wouldn't even lift his toe off the floor. I got the oil on, got him in the stall, fed him and left. That's why I'm so late."

Her mother came through the doorway with a tray

of food. "Is that why you're so dirty, too?"

Jackie looked down at her jeans. There were oil spots where she had been kneeling in the hoof dressing and mud where she had splashed through a stream.

"I suggest you clean up before your father sees you."

"Okay." Jackie ran down the hall and into her bedroom, where she pulled a clean tee shirt from her drawer and another pair of jeans from the closet, then ran into the bathroom.

Her father didn't exactly object to her interest in horses, but neither was he wildly enthusiastic. He thought she would be better off doing something less expensive, like swimming, where all he would be required to provide was a bathing suit. But over the two years she had been riding, Jackie had managed to acquire the clothes and equipment she needed.

Except a horse. Her father had said it was out of the question, every time the subject had come up, and sometimes mentioned it even when the subject hadn't come up. Horses were too expensive. After buying it, there was feed and the vet and the blacksmith, and to his mind, it never stopped, so he vowed it would never start.

The Griffins were on a treadmill, Mr. Knapp said. They bought Moose for Lisa and within two years she wanted a fancier horse to take to shows. She wasn't satisfied with just riding around town, she wanted to go places and needed a horse trailer and better clothes. Mr. Knapp wanted no part of that.

All Jackie wanted was a horse. She wanted to ride. Even if she couldn't go to the bigger shows, there were local 4-H shows, where just a plain horse would not be frowned upon. Lisa had always said Jackie's horse could go with them, if Jackie ever got a horse of her own.

Now she only had Moose. Lisa let Jackie take care of Moose for her 4-H project, which required the member only to care for the horse, not own it. Moose was nearly twenty years old now, and slow and fat. But he was a horse she could care for and ride.

In the good weather, the 4-H members met at someone's riding ring, and their leader, Fiona Jaegger, gave them a group lesson. It wasn't funny to anyone anymore that Moose would always knock over even the smallest jump Fiona set up, that he wouldn't canter on his left lead, that he galloped as fast as everyone else trotted and always wound up bringing up the rear on a trail ride. But he was something to ride, and he was a horse; Jackie felt fortunate for that much. Lisa didn't have to let her take care of Moose, although Lisa didn't want to do the extra work and he was so old the family didn't want to sell him. Everyone benefited from the arrangement.

Jackie came back into the dining room, looking far more respectable, and sat down at the table. Her father, sitting at the head of the table, glanced over her appraisingly, which made her glad she had changed clothes.

"I suppose you were over at Griffin's again today," he said.

"Yes, I was," she answered unsurely. He knew perfectly well she went there every day after school.

"I've always told you I wouldn't buy you a horse."

"Yes, sir, I know that." The picture of her own horse standing at the doorway to the shed, which stood in their small orchard, faded in her mind.

"I was hoping you were going to get over this horse-craziness before long."

She wished he wouldn't treat her feelings about horses so lightly. She loved them, and she was going to keep on loving them. A week, a month or a year wasn't going to change her mind. But she knew better than to try to explain that to him; his mind was set.

"I suppose you are going to keep on riding, whatever I say."

"I'm not going to give it up, if I have a choice."

"I surmised as much," he said wryly. "Mr. Maher was speaking with me today. His daughter, Joanne, is leaving for college in September, and they have to get rid of that horse of theirs. Bob wants to sell it, but his daughter says she would rather give it away to someone who really wants a horse and can't afford to buy one. I said we'd take the horse."

"Dad!"

"Only if you meet with her approval. She wants the horse to go to someone who is going to love it and take care of it the way she has. She doesn't want it going to a stable, where it wouldn't be able to go out every day or might be mistreated; she's had it since it was young."

"Perfect! He could live in the shed and come in and go out whenever he pleased, and I already know how to take care of a horse. I've been taking care of Moose for almost a year."

"You'll have chores to do first thing in the morning, even before you go to school. It won't be easy, I'm sure."

"How hard could it be? I think it's great!"

"I don't know how great it's going to be, but I told Mr. Maher to have his daughter call tonight so she can speak directly to you."

"Wonderful!"

"Please, Jackie, finish your dinner before you get carried away," her mother admonished.

"How can I eat at a time like this?"

"Try," Mr. Knapp prompted.

The telephone rang in the kitchen.

"It must be her!" Jackie exclaimed, jumping up from her chair, which tipped over. She picked it up and ran into the kitchen, slid on the linoleum until she bumped into the wall, and picked up the phone. "Hello?"

"Hello. This is Joanne Maher. May I speak to Jackie?"

"This is me. I'm her. I mean, I'm Jackie."

"Hi." The girl at the other end laughed. "My father says you're interested in horses."

"I'm in love with horses. I'd be in paradise if I had my own horse to take care of."

"That's what my dad said. I can just imagine our two fathers moaning to each other at work about their horse-crazy daughters. I'd like to come over and see where Charlie would live. I've had him since he was three, and I couldn't let him go to someone I didn't know. I can't keep him any longer. I'll be away in college, and it wouldn't be fair to Charlie to keep him standing in the backyard while I'm away, and besides, my parents don't want to take care of him for the next four years. My father thought I should sell him, but I'd rather give him to someone I know would love him and take care of him the way I have. I wouldn't want him being sold and eventually winding up at a hack stable where he'd be rented out by the hour all day long. Charlie's always had special attention, and I thought if I could find some young girl who was like I was when I was twelve or so, it would be just the place for Charlie."

"I've been in a 4-H club for two years and have

been taking care of one of my friend's horses since September, and I know the right way to take care of a horse. I know about grooming and feeding and cleaning the stall, and if I don't know, I can always call our club leader and ask."

"It sounds pretty good. If it's convenient for you, I'll drive over Saturday afternoon and take a look around. Then we can talk in person. And I'll give you an idea of what Charlie's like and what you'll have to do for him."

"Saturday's just fine with me. I'll make sure I finish with Moose in plenty of time."

"Fine. I'll be there around two. See you then."

"Okay. Thank you. Good-bye." Jackie said and hung the phone back on its cradle. She stood there for a moment, not believing her luck.

She was going to have a horse of her own. If Joanne approved of the shed and the orchard and herself, she, Jackie Knapp, would be able to ride her own horse to the lessons and trail rides the club held. And maybe if she worked very hard all summer, she would be able to take Charlie to the 4-H Fair in August, and that was the most important 4-H horse show for the entire year.

Charlie. A horse named Charlie just had to be perfect in every way.

Chapter Two

JACKIE FELT AS IF SHE HAD GOTTEN TEN BIRTHDAYS and six Christmases all rolled into one ever since Joanne had agreed to let her have Charlie. The pasture was good, the shed was all right, and Joanne actually trusted Jackie to take care of Charlie properly. It was all Jackie could do to sit still in school, she was so excited about the prospect of having a horse of her very own. It was all she could talk about; she and Lisa had made enough plans for a year's worth of riding. There were horse shows to go to, hunter paces to ride, places to explore. Jackie had even decided that Charlie's stable colors were going to be red and gray. Lisa had a way of turning two regular people blankets into a horse cooler, and Jackie was going to make one for Charlie for Christmas. A big red cooler, bound in gray, with Charlie in white letters sewn onto the left flank.

She could hardly wait to tell Fiona. The news was going to surprise her, for sure. Fiona, Jackie had always thought, didn't treat her seriously because she didn't have a horse of her own. Jackie had been the only member of the club who didn't have her own horse, but now that was going to be different. Fiona was going to see for herself that it wasn't Jackie's riding that was at fault, it was Moose who wasn't being cooperative when they didn't do what Fiona asked during the lessons.

Fiona was going to have to change her opinion of Jackie and realize that she could be a good rider. All the silly business they had been going through in the lessons would be over when Jackie and Charlie trotted into the ring and floated around a gigantic course of fences. Fiona's mouth was going to drop open in amazement when she saw that performance. She would say, "Jackie, I never suspected you were such a good rider. With a little bit of work, though not much really, you'll be riding with the top juniors in no time. Maybe you should find yourself another teacher who can help you. There's not much more that I can teach you." Fiona would walk away shaking her head.

Jackie could see it happening.

On Wednesday, she and Lisa raced to get Moose and Ginger Ale ready to ride to their weekly lesson. They trotted in the dirt beside the road to get there early, so Jackie would have time before the lesson to tell Fiona. When they arrived at the ring, they learned that Fiona was inside talking with Mrs. Antenucci, so Lisa went off to ride Ginger Ale outside the ring, and Jackie stayed inside and kept walking Moose around, waiting.

"Fiona!" Jackie called as soon as she saw her coming up to the ring from the house. "I've got wonderful news!"

Fiona smiled and entered the ring by sliding herself between the rails of the fence. "What is it, Jackie, or should I guess?"

"Guess."

"You're getting a horse."

"How'd you know?" Jackie said, disappointed.

Fiona laughed. "What else could it be? Your face is lit up like a jack-o-lantern on Halloween."

"By next lesson, I'll have Charlie. That's his name, and I won't be stuck with Moose anymore."

Fiona patted Moose's shoulder. "Give this poor guy some credit. He's all right."

"He's a slow-poke, and you know it."

"I know he's old, but I also know you could get more out of him if you tried a little harder."

Jackie fidgeted in the saddle. "I won't have to

worry about that anymore."

"Oh, you won't."

Lisa trotted over on Ginger Ale and stood beside Moose. "No, really, Fiona. This Charlie is a show horse."

"Really."

Fiona wasn't going to take their word for it, Jackie knew. She always treated everything like a story. "It's true. He's won all kinds of ribbons."

"What's his name?"

Jackie thought for a moment. All she knew him by was Charlie. She didn't know if he had a show name that was different from his stable name as some horses did. "Charlie, I guess," she answered.

"How come I've never heard of him."

"Because he lives out by Hartford and never showed around here. But Lisa and I are going to show all the time. Maybe this year we'll even start hitting recognized shows."

Fiona raised her eyebrows.

"Jackie would be ready if she had a better horse than Moose, don't you think so, Fiona?" Lisa asked.

Fiona looked from Jackie to Lisa and back to Jackie, then shook her head. "What makes you think I'm a fortune-teller? If Jackie worked hard and this horse was pretty good, maybe she could show in some simple recognized shows this year."

"See!" Jackie and Lisa said triumphantly in unison.

"Wait a minute. That means a lot of hard work, Jackie. You know you haven't been riding as long as Lisa, and you do tend to lay back instead of being aggressive."

"I won't have to worry about that anymore. Charlie is perfectly trained and will do anything I ask. His owner said so. He's a real gentleman, and I know I won't have the slightest trouble with him. Lisa and I are going to be a team for the hunter pace in the fall, aren't we?"

"Sure," Lisa answered, nodding.

"I wish you'd slow down a bit and see what happens. This horse might turn out to be a real turkey."

"A turkey! He's the horse of my dreams. He's so beautiful. A bright red chestnut with a blaze face and two white socks. You should see him."

"So you've ridden him already?"

Jackie paused. "No, not yet. I didn't really have time to get up to see him. Joanne has to leave for Colorado and has all these things to do, and my parents just didn't have time this week to drive me all the way up there."

"It sounds like a mistake to me. You should ride the horse before you get committed," Fiona said seriously.

"But I saw picture of him. And I couldn't ask for anything more. He's really a fantastic horse. He came in fifth in some big show Joanne took him to a while back. Beat all kinds of thoroughbreds. He's practically an open jumper, he's so fantastic."

Fiona burst into laughter. "I want to see it with my own eyes before I'm going to believe a word of this. He sounds too good to be true."

"He's not. He's perfect, and he's the answer to all my dreams. I can't believe how lucky I am. I mean, it would have been great to get any horse, but to get Charlie, who is so beautiful and talented! What could be better?"

Fiona smiled. "I don't know, but I have a feeling I should wait to decide. Now why don't you really make Moose work today, and we'll get on with this lesson." She began walking to the center of the ring, then turned back. "I'm glad you got a horse, Jackie. But I just have the feeling that you don't realize what a responsibility it is having a horse."

"I take care of Moose."

"That's not the same as having your own, at your house. Having a horse is more than just riding. It's ninety percent work. And it's going to be hard."

"I don't mind working hard just as long as I have a horse of my very own."

"I know you'll do the work. I know you'll take care of him, but it's more than that. It's an attitude you get about having a horse. I can't explain it to you. You'll have to find out for yourself. I just don't want you to get discouraged."

"Why would I get discouraged? I'm getting a horse after waiting a million years. He's super-perf. What could go wrong?"

Fiona closed her eyes and got a pained expression on her face. "If you can ask that, you don't know, you poor kid. Well," Fiona tilted her head jauntily and saluted, "welcome to the club and hold onto your hat. You're in for the ride of your life."

Jackie and Lisa watched as Fiona walked out into the center of the ring.

"What did she mean?" Jackie asked.

"I don't know."

"Why does Fiona always talk in riddles?"

"I don't know."

"Were you discouraged after you got Ginger?"

"No."

"I don't get it."

"Don't let it bother you. Fiona always sees trouble where there isn't any. You know that."

"Yeah. She can see problems everywhere. Charlie's not going to be a problem. Everything is going to be perfect."

"Sure," Lisa agreed, and they both kicked their horses forward to join the lesson.

Chapter
Three

JACKIE SAT ON THE FRONT STEP WAITING FOR THE trailer with Charlie to come down the road and into her yard. She had worked on his stall for over five days to make it comfortable for him. Once Joanne had decided to let Charlie come to live with them, the shed had been remodeled so there would be a stall and a small tack room, which would hold all her tack as well as feed, and pitchforks, shovels and maintenance equipment. The orchard fence had been improved for horse use, as directed by Joanne. Even Jackie's father had seemed to enjoy all the activity, although he had never said so. With some oil paints left over from a set, Jackie had painted Charlie's name on a smooth piece of wood and nailed it over the stall door. And now everything was ready.

Lisa would have been there with Jackie, but she had gone to a show for the day. But Jackie didn't mind waiting alone. It gave her time to think and plan. She still couldn't believe her luck. She was going to have her own horse! In her mind, she could see them galloping across the fields and jumping stone walls; nothing would be too much. She would be able to ride him in the 4-H Fair and have a decent chance to collect some ribbons.

Jackie's mother had asked Joanne if Charlie might get wild sometimes and maybe throw Jackie off, but Joanne had told them that Charlie would never think of such a thing. Of course not, Jackie thought. Charlie had manners. He wasn't the common type horse; she had known that just by looking at the picture Joanne had shown her. He wasn't going to be like Moose who wouldn't let her catch him in the pasture. Charlie wasn't going to turn and trot away, no. He would probably wait right there for her and let her snap the lead rope onto his halter. Or better yet, he'd come as soon as he saw her standing at his stall door. That was manners. She wouldn't have to struggle to pick up his feet to clean them. Even Joanne said he was a real gentleman to work around. He wasn't the type to raise his head so high no one could reach it to put the bridle on, and he wouldn't keep his teeth clenched shut to avoid the bit. And he wouldn't be afraid of getting water on him, like Moose, who tried to get away every time someone came near him with a hose. Charlie knew about baths, and he wasn't going to act up about that.

It was fantastic enough that she was getting a horse, but that she was getting a super one like Charlie seemed almost impossible. She would have been glad to have Moose for her own, even with all the problems he caused, but taking care of Charlie was going to be simple with the kind of cooperation he would give her.

In another few weeks, she would be out of school for the summer, and she would be able to devote all day to Charlie. Grooming, cleaning the stall, soaping the tack Joanne was going to leave with her, and then riding. There would be the lessons with the other club members each week. It was going to be the best summer of her whole life. Even better than the year she had gone to camp for a month and ridden every other day. Of course, the horses there were school horses, not the same caliber as Charlie, or as Lisa's Ginger Ale. Besides all she had done at summer camp was to trot around and around the little ring, and once they had gone on a short trail ride. At the time she had thought it was wonderful, but now she knew better. That kind of riding was just for people who didn't care about being a good rider.

She really did want to ride properly, not just get

on and gallop away. She liked the idea of going to horse shows, even though she had only ridden in two with Moose at the 4-H grounds, and she hadn't done very well. But she hadn't had so many lessons then, and she rode Moose much better now.

There would be a chance for her to win at shows with Charlie; the rest of the club members would see then that it hadn't been her fault that things always seemed to go wrong with Moose. Maybe with Charlie she would be able to make it into the finals of the Fair Challenge Trophy class. That was the biggest class, and winning that was just as good as winning the championship. Of course, she would be competing against older riders, too, in the class. But nothing would be impossible with Charlie.

Joanne would never be sorry she left Charlie with her, Jackie was certain. He couldn't have any better care even if he went to live at the most beautiful stable in the whole country, not even if he had two grooms standing there all day waiting to serve him.

A red pickup truck turned into their driveway pulling a red trailer, and Jackie jumped up from the step. She ran to the front door, opened it and called, "He's here, Mom!" She raced to the driveway just as the truck was coming to a halt.

Joanne got out of the truck and came around the back of the trailer, stood on the ramp hinges and looked in at Charlie, then patted his rump. "You're at

your new home, Charlie. I'll have you out in a minute. Dick, if you get the ramp, I'll back him out."

The young man who had driven the truck nodded
and went to the ramp's handles. Joanne went to the
side door of the trailer, went inside, and soon had
Charlie ready to get out. "Okay."

"You're set?" Dick asked, holding the last handle,
already having let the ramp down; all that stopped
Charlie was a small gate.

"Let 'er rip," Joanne answered.

Dick opened the gate, and Charlie took the first
slow steps backward, followed by several fast steps

until he was on the ground with his head up scanning the unfamiliar scenery. Joanne followed him out, holding onto his lead rope.

"Charlie sometimes has a bad time in a trailer, so I'll leave all his bandages and leg wraps with you. A horse really shouldn't travel without protection. And don't forget to put his bell boots on."

Jackie glanced down and saw the four white protective rubber boots covering Charlie's hooves. These were partially covered by thick white fleecy material, which was wrapped from the hooves all the way to just below his knees and held in place by flannel leg bandages. It was more padding than Jackie had ever seen.

"I've seen too many accidents to risk not bandaging legs. All a horse has to do is lose his balance and step one hoof down on the other and that can be a serious injury."

"We were taught about bandaging in 4-H, and I promise he'll never go near a trailer without being wrapped."

"I know you won't. You're a good kid. Charlie didn't have a bad ride at all today, did he, Dick?"

"Nope. It was a good trip," he said slapping Charlie's rump as he walked past to raise the ramp.

Charlie looked around the yard for a few seconds, then dropped his head to nibble at the grass by the drive. Joanne patted his sweaty neck. "I guess it was pretty warm in the trailer for him."

Jackie guessed it was because his cotton sheet was soaked, and not only was he foamy on the neck, there was sweat dripping from his belly.

Charlie took a few steps, nearly pulling Joanne with him, and she laughed. "Charlie is a compulsive eater. You won't have any trouble keeping weight on him. If you feed him what I've written down, he'll stay in perfect condition."

"We already have a supply in. The oats are the same brand you've had, and we've called a farmer in town who will sell us hay."

"Make sure it's horse hay not the stuff for cows. Sometimes hay can be poor in quality and that doesn't do much for a horse. Charlie won't eat some hays, but if it's good, he'll finish it right up."

"The man said it was timothy and clover with some . . . I forget what he said."

"Alfalfa?"

"That was it."

"That's a good standard mixture. Don't feed him dusty or moldy hay, but I guess you know that from 4-H, don't you?"

"Yes."

"Here," Joanne said, holding out the lead rope. "He's all yours now. Take care of him."

"I will, I promise."

"I'll be away most of the summer, but maybe I'll

stop in before I go off to school. I hope you won't mind if I drop in every once in a while for a visit."

"No, come whenever you want, I'm sure Charlie would want to see you."

"Good. Why don't I help you take off his wraps, put him in his new home, and I'll get going before I start crying."

Jackie felt so sorry for Joanne that she could have cried, too. How awful it was to be leaving her horse with a stranger, a horse who had been hers for years and years. Jackie never wanted to go through that; she was going to keep Charlie until he was old and gray. Now that she finally had a horse, she was never going to part with him.

They walked to the pasture, where Jackie unsnapped the lead, and Charlie went a few steps on his own then put his head down and began cropping the grass.

"I guess he's not going to have a difficult time adjusting to it here. It's so nice and peaceful. You did a good job on the fence," Joanne commented pointing to the new section of post and rails, then continued through the orchard until she reached the shed. "This looks good, too. It's a roomy box stall." She glanced in the doorway, then looked back at Jackie for a long moment. "I know I'm being a real jerk about this horse, but I'm going to miss him, even if he's not going to miss me."

"I'm sure he'll miss you."

Joanne smiled. "For a while maybe. But you'll keep him so busy, he won't have a chance to think about anything else. I've had him so long, he seems like a part of me. I haven't had a morning in years when I didn't have to get up extra early to take care of Charlie. Sometimes it was more trouble than I wanted right then, but mostly I felt like I wasn't doing work, that I was giving someone something they couldn't do for themselves. I'm leaving."

Jackie stood there while Joanne turned to walk away.

"I forgot to mention it, but Charlie didn't get his shots yet for this year so you'd better have the vet come by and do that for him. He's your responsibility now."

Jackie nodded and looked over to Charlie. His back was towards her, his tail swishing back and forth. Joanne walked up to him, kissed his nose and hurried out of the pasture. Within a few seconds, the truck and trailer were pulling out down the driveway. Jackie sat down on a big rock underneath an apple tree; she was just going to sit there and watch her horse.

Chapter Four

Jackie was riding Charlie alongside the road towards Lisa's house. Her mother hadn't wanted her to take such a long ride before she was really used to Charlie, but Jackie had explained that the vet was going to be at Lisa's and if Jackie could get Charlie over there, the two families could split the cost of the visit, making both bills smaller. Her father had seen the sense of that and had said she could go if she was careful.

Charlie was no trouble to get tacked up. He did come right up to her in the pasture and stood tied to the shed without fussing while she brushed him carefully, cleaned his hooves and then put all his tack on. He opened his mouth to take the bit practically before she had the bit in place, and he didn't blow his stomach full of air so she had difficulty tightening the girth.

She could hardly wait for the next riding lesson so everyone in the club could see her new horse. Sleek and beautiful, Charlie had a white star and strip down his bright chestnut face. Even in her wildest dreams, she couldn't have imagined having such a pretty horse. He was every bit as attractive as Lisa's Ginger Ale, who was a very nice-looking horse.

And she knew that with as much training as he had had, she would have no problems with him in the riding lessons. Her problem days were over. She was riding Charlie on a loose rein along the road, and he wasn't straying or trying to walk faster or slower or grab at leaves. He wasn't even afraid of the storm drains, which were practically guaranteed to startle any horse. Charlie just walked right around them without looking or skittering at the sound of water running in them.

They turned up Lisa's drive, which was a long dirt road because at one time the land had been a huge dairy farm. Mr. Griffin had converted the barn to accommodate horses instead of cows, and some of the land had been sold, but there were still acres of pasture and a nice pond they used for swimming in the summer and skating in the winter. And Lisa had a ring to ride in if she didn't want to ride off the farm.

Mr. Griffin had more money to spend on Lisa than Jackie's father had because he was an airline pilot, and everyone knew they were paid really well. Plus he was almost always home because pilots shouldn't get tired out and start falling asleep at the controls. But today he was away. Jackie always wanted to know where he was, but Lisa hardly ever knew. It was always someplace far away like Caracas or Munich or Tangiers. The Griffins didn't think that was anything special or out of the ordinary, just as Lisa didn't think it was any big deal to have her own trailer and a father who was glad to drive her any-place she wanted to go, providing he was around to do it.

When Jackie got up to the house, she saw that there were two carpenters up on the roof of the screened-in porch. There was all kinds of lumber on the ground and a couple of rolls of pink fiberglass in-sulation, looking like cotton candy wrapped up in aluminum foil. The porch was going to be glassed-in, and they were going to get an old-style Franklin stove so they could sit out there in the winter. Parked behind the house, almost at the woods, were a truck and trailer, and the bulldozer that went with them was pushing dirt around. Charlie surveyed everything with casual interest, and the minute she jumped off, he put his head down and started reaching for grass.

She pulled his head up with some difficulty and

brought him over to the barn. Lisa came out, pushing the wheelbarrow.

"Why don't you put Charlie out in the first pasture. I have the fence blocked off so we won't have to go running through the fields to chase them when Dr. Mielzener comes."

Jackie untacked Charlie and put on the halter she had brought with her, then turned him out. Lisa was waiting for her at the manure pile.

"There sure is a lot of work here now that you're not taking care of Moose anymore. It seems as if I never get finished."

"That's because you work so slow. If you got right down to business, it wouldn't take you any time at all."

"I still have to do two stalls a day, and that's plenty of work."

"If you haven't finished, I'll help you."

"Good. I was hoping you'd say that."

"Is that why you waited until I got here to start cleaning up?"

"Yup."

Jackie laughed. "It figures." They both went into the barn, which was dark and cool even with the windows open letting the warm breeze in. Jackie took one step into Moose's stall and knew that Lisa hadn't given it a decent cleaning for the past week. "I'd love you to get a spot check from Fiona right now. You'd get a D in barn management. Anyone can tell you haven't done this stall in days."

"I have so," Lisa protested. "But you know what a slob Moose is. He waits until he comes inside before he messes. It's the reverse of housebroken."

Taking a manure fork, Jackie began working on Moose's stall while Lisa began sweeping down the aisle. "Why don't you have the lights on?"

Lisa was up at the other end and it was so far that Jackie could hardly hear her. "I think the carpenters are messing with the wires or something. When I hit the switch, it was dead. And boy, isn't it dark in here?"

"It sure is. I hope the vet can see what he's doing."

"We'll have to do it outside. No point in working inside anyway. He just has to give them a shot. The tetanus and the encephalitis are combined, I think. Or is it . . ."

"I think you're right, but last spring is so long ago, I forget."

Lisa was down at Jackie's end, pushing the wide-headed broom, then stopped. "I think I hear a truck coming, but with all that banging up on the roof and that bulldozer out back, I can't tell."

Jackie poked her head out the stall door and saw the vet's truck come up the drive and park by the house. She put the fork up against the wall and walked outside with Lisa.

"Hi, Dr. Mielzener. This is Jackie, you know her, and her horse is that chestnut." Lisa pointed out toward the small pasture alongside the barn.

"Hi, Jackie," the doctor answered, opening a compartment in the truck and reaching inside for his black bag. "How is everyone around here?"

"Ginger's fine, but Moose is such a pig," Lisa answered.

He laughed. "I'm sorry, Lisa, but I'm all out of pig pills today. What are we doing, spring shots?"

"That's right."

He walked over toward the barn, paying particular attention to the activity on the room and in the backyard. "You really shouldn't wait until summer before you take the notion to call."

"I know. I kept meaning to call and I kept forgetting, but it's not too late, is it?"

"Almost. What's all this building? Constructing a new house?"

"Just a different porch. Who do you want first?" Lisa asked swinging a lead rope around her in a circle.

"Ginger, I guess," he said as if it didn't matter to him and that was the first name that came into his head.

Lisa went out into the pasture, and Jackie stood there with her hands in her back pockets.

"How long have you had that chestnut horse?" Dr. Mielzener asked.

"Almost a week. His name is Charlie."

"Um. Is he a nice, quiet horse?"

"Yes," she answered. "Why?"

He shrugged. "I get worried when people your size get hot horses that might not be safe for them."

"Charlie's safe. He was trained by a girl who's going to college and he's wonderful to work around, especially after Moose."

"That's right. You were taking care of him this past year."

"I was, and it's great having Charlie. I can even pick his feet up by myself."

"Have you ridden him much?"

"Sure, every day since I got him. Just by my house mostly. So we could get used to each other, and he's really good. Trots right off when you ask him. I haven't cantered him yet. I thought I'd save that for when I could go on a trail or maybe ride in the ring. I don't have room for a ring at my house. Charlie just lives in this little orchard we have, and it's perfect for him; but with all the trees, I can't ride out there."

Lisa came up to them with Ginger Ale, who was just about that color. "I don't think we can do it in the barn. The electricity is off, and you know how dark it is in there."

"Okay. It doesn't make any difference to me; it'll only take a second anyway." He put his bag down on the ground by the barn, removed a needle, syringe and a bottle of yellowish liquid. "Why don't you go out and get Charlie. We'll be done by the time you get back."

"All right," Jackie said, and taking a lead rope with her, she headed for the pasture where both Moose and Charlie were standing watching Ginger Ale intently.

Jackie liked Dr. Mielzener. He was young, just out of vet school a few years, and was the younger partner of an older veterinarian. But Dr. Mielzener wasn't like a regular vet. He wore a floppy hat wherever he went, and he clumped around in gigantic boots all the time. He wore coveralls that were too big for him, and he had long curly hair. Jackie thought he looked more like someone from the backwoods than from the University of Pennsylvania, and he never cared what time people called him if their animals were in trouble. He hadn't even minded when Lisa called to tell him that Moose had just eaten the aluminum foil wrapper from a potato sticks bag.

Jackie patted Charlie on the neck and snapped the lead rope onto his halter. "This is pretty interesting for you, isn't it? I know you're not going to be a fool like Moose. Look at how well Ginger Ale is doing." She opened the gate, led him through, then turned him around so she could get the gate closed before Moose could come with them. By the time she reached the barn, Lisa passed them going back towards the pasture. "See how easy it is. It's just a little pinprick, and Moose always has to act as if we're trying to drain away every drop of blood. You know, Charlie, there is nothing I like more than a sensible horse." She stood him on the drive and kissed his nose.

The doctor was back by the barn getting another needle and syringe, so Jackie stood holding the end of the rope and Charlie stood there watching the vet with his ears pricked forward.

"Looks like it's going to be an easy day for me," Dr. Mielzener said coming closer to them.

"I hope Moose doesn't act up for you," Jackie said, just as Charlie began to take a couple of steps, pulling her off balance. "Hey, Charlie. Come here."

Jackie took a tighter grip of the lead rope with her left hand and grabbed hold of his halter with her right. "Forget about the grass for five minutes and stand still."

The vet reached the driveway, and Charlie started walking away, pulling Jackie with him. "Hey, what's going on, Charlie?"

"Here, let me help you. I'll get him." Dr. Mielzener came over to the left side and took hold of the rope just where it clipped onto the halter, and Jackie had both hands at the end of the cotton lead rope.

Charlie just kept on walking, and even when Jackie tried to lean back with all her weight and her feet braced, she was going along and so was Dr. Mielzener.

Once Charlie realized they weren't going to stop him from walking, he picked up speed and started to jog.

"Charlie. Stop!" Jackie told him, running to keep up. That was all he needed. He started to trot, fast, and Jackie had to really run to keep up with him.

The three of them hit the grass, and Jackie found herself struggling to stay upright and to keep from stepping on the doctor at the same time. She tried bracing her feet again and started sliding on the grass, which was still wet from the dew.

Charlie just kept pulling them along, trotting progressively faster. The doctor had better traction than she did, with his big black rubber boots on, and he

kept running, but by the time they reached the well, Jackie had to let go because the rope had been pulled right through her hands. She stood there watching the vet go up toward the woods, not running anymore but skiing behind Charlie.

Then she saw what was going to happen if the vet didn't stop Charlie. He was headed right for the bulldozer, and the driver obviously didn't see him. Jackie turned toward the pasture. "Lisa! Come quick!"

Lisa was already running toward the gate, and both Moose and Ginger Ale were running around like crazy; they could see Charlie running free because the vet had let go at the edge of the yard.

"Lisa! You go toward the pasture, I'll cut him off

toward the house!" Jackie didn't want him running down the side of the property and out toward the road, so she ran as fast as she could, keeping her eye on Charlie while she raced around the back of the house. She maneuvered by the lumber and skirted the little white fence, until she heard one crack, then another, and the next thing she knew she was sitting in a mound of soft dirt with her right foot under her. She had fallen into one of the ruts the bulldozer had made when it went through the yard.

"I broke my ankle!" she cried out. There was no doubt in her mind, even though she had never broken anything before. Her ankle had gone crack-crack, and that could only mean one thing. She was going to be laid up all summer.

Dr. Mielzener looked at her from across the yard, then at Charlie, who was going to meet his fate in a duel with the bulldozer within seconds, trying to decide who to go for. He turned back to her and ran over. Crouching beside her, he felt her ankle then told her to stand. "It's not broken," he pronounced, but she couldn't put her weight on it.

The sound of the bulldozer stopped, suddenly, and in a minute the man who was running it brought Charlie up to them. His face was about the color of Charlie's star. "This horse nearly gave me a heart attack. I never saw him coming, and then he's in front of my 'dozer."

Jackie limped a couple of steps, leaning against Lisa, then looked around. There was laughter coming from someplace. Peals of laughter. She glanced up and saw the two carpenters up on the roof doubled over with laughter, their faces bright red, even through their dark tans.

"What are they laughing at?" Jackie whispered to Lisa.

"Fools will laugh at anything."

One of the carpenters came down the ladder, his body still shaking. "Need some help?" he asked, wiping tears from his eyes.

"I guess it wouldn't hurt," Dr. Mielzener said, holding onto the left side of Charlie's halter; the dozer man was holding the lead rope.

"I know something about animals," the carpenter said with conviction. "I was brought up on a farm, and I always rode bareback."

Lisa looked at Jackie and raised her eyebrows. "Oh sure. I'll just bet he did. What's that got to do with this?"

The carpenter grabbed the right side of the halter, and that seemed to be Charlie's signal. He began to move again, and this time he was pulling three men across the yard. It didn't seem to be any problem at all for Charlie. He was big and strong and had bulging muscles all over his body. The three men had to struggle to keep up with him.

"Head him towards the white fence. We'll stop him there," Dr. Mielzener called to the others, while Lisa and Jackie just stood and watched in amazement.

"Okay," the other two called back, and the three of them shifted everything they had to the left to prevent Charlie from going back around the front of the house.

The way Charlie was going, Jackie didn't think a little picket fence, which was only for decoration and stood about two feet six inches, was going to do a thing to stop him. And she was right.

Charlie didn't stop at the fence. With one leap he jumped right over it, bringing everyone with him. It didn't even slow him down. The dozer man had the most trouble because he was holding onto the lead rope, not the halter like the vet and the carpenter. So he had to jump the fence by himself, and since he was a little on the chunky side, he just made it, holding onto the rope with one hand.

Lisa's hands were covering her face. "I can't watch," she said as Charlie headed for the big stack of lumber. "Tell me when it's over."

"Left," Dr. Mielzener called, and again everyone swung left, just enough to miss the two by fours, but not enough to miss the two rolls of insulation. They went right over that; the dozer man running around it to avoid having to go over the top like the others.

"Head him toward the pasture fence," the vet called, and by digging in, they all managed to direct Charlie behind the barn and corner him at the fence. Once they had him pointed toward the wall, even Charlie knew he had to admit defeat. He stopped. Everyone stopped. The three men wiped their faces and shook their heads.

Lisa removed her hands from her face. "Did he stop?"

"Yes." Jackie sighed with relief and started hobbling over to him. Moose was running around the pasture with his tail up, snorting like a locomotive. "Oh, shut up, Moose. You're no help at all."

With everyone holding on and blocking his escape, the doctor was able to give Charlie his shot quickly, then patted him.

"I'm sorry, Dr. Mielzener," Jackie apologized. "Charlie is always such a gentleman. I don't know what made him act like such an idiot. I'm sorry he dragged you through the yard."

Dr. Mielzener looked Charlie square in the face. "It's nothing. Matter of fact, I kind of like this horse," he said.

The carpenter and the dozer man sat down on the grass to rest, every once in a while looking at Charlie in disbelief.

But Jackie just looked at Dr. Mielzener. She didn't

know how he could say he liked Charlie after all they had been through. She wasn't sure she could say that much herself, at least not right then.

"What am I going to do with you, Charlie?" she asked him as he eyed her with his ears pricked forward. He looked so cute, she had to put her arms around his neck.

"Don't worry about it, Jackie," Dr. Mielzener said. "If you can still find it in your heart to love him now, you'll work out all your problems eventually. People who can't bounce back don't last long with horses. It must be a case of natural selection. The fittest of us stick with it. And with a face like Charlie's, who could resist."

"Are you sure?" she asked dismally.

"I'm positive," he said optimistically. "Would I mislead you? No. Now who's going to get Moose for me? After all, there are other horses scheduled to bite, kick and/or chase me through soggy pastures today. I can't stay here relaxing in the sunshine. I have work to do."

Jackie was willling to take his word for it. She was already crazy about Charlie. And she got to thinking that if this was the worst he could be, it wasn't so bad after all.

She even had to smile as she remembered Charlie jumping the three men over the picket fence. It took a horse with some class to do that, and Charlie had more than a little class. Charlie had more class in one strand of his mane than Moose had in his mane and tail together. And Moose had the bushiest mane and tail of any horse she had ever seen.

Chapter
Five

Fiona studied Charlie. She looked in his mouth, at his feet and his eyes. Jackie thought the only place Fiona hadn't looked was down Charlie's throat, and that wouldn't be easy because it was so dark down there.

"He looks like a pretty nice horse," she pronounced finally. "How does he go?"

"I haven't had a chance to find out because he just got his shots a few days ago, then when I could ride, it rained. Today is the first time I'm going to try to do anything with him."

"Is he quiet? He won't kick at anyone?"

"I don't think so. He's really good on the road.

Just walks right along, doesn't mind the cars or the bikes passing him."

"That's a relief. We don't need another kicker in the club."

Jackie nodded in agreement. Linda Nicholas's horse, Diablo, would kick at anyone who got too close. Linda always rode at the end of a trail ride, and she always found herself isolated in the lessons because almost everyone had been kicked by her gelding at least once. Jackie had gotten it in the foot when Moose came up too close and Diablo had sashayed into position to let him have it and got her instead. Diablo always bucked after every fence, too, unseating Linda every time.

Nina Torielli came up to Jackie on her dark brown pony. "Is that Charlie?"

"Yes."

"He's cute. You were really lucky to get him for free. I heard all about it from Lisa's mother down at the feed store."

It was impossible to keep anything secret from the club. Someone would always start blabbing. "Yeah. I was lucky."

"Okay, Lisa. That's enough jumping. If everyone is here, let's start the lesson. I want to get down to the beach," Fiona announced.

Fiona liked the beach. She stayed there nearly all

summer, roasting first on one side, then the other, with grease all over her. Jackie and Lisa had been down there once when Fiona was there, so they knew. And the thought of it made Jackie wrinkle her nose. All that grease would make her feel slimy. But for that quirk, Fiona was a good leader for the club. She took them interesting places, like a saddle factory and a breeding farm and a farm where they raised miniature horses. And Fiona knew about horses, too, and could ride herself. Jackie thought that was very important. But they didn't do much in the summer because Fiona was on the beach. She was available to help them prepare their yearly record books for entry in the 4-H Fair and give the weekly lesson, but they didn't go any place as a group.

"Okay, everyone, let's have a nice strong trot," Fiona called to them, and everyone began fussing with their reins because they hadn't been ready.

Jackie wasn't sure how Charlie was going to react to having eight horses in the ring with him, but she nudged him with her legs, and he went into his nice slow trot.

"Faster, Jackie. Don't let Charlie dawdle. We want a hunter trot, not a western jog."

Jackie squeezed again, and Charlie just kept going along at the same speed, hugging the rail, not paying the slightest attention to anyone in the ring.

"Wake up, Jackie. Let's get moving out there," Fiona said.

She nudged Charlie harder and still got no response. People were beginning to pass her because Jackie was going much slower than they were. Charlie was really going only a little bit faster than a walk, while everyone else was doing a full-fledged trot. Jackie kept working at him while Fiona commented on the others, and she finally got him up to speed. Then Fiona told them to walk and reverse.

Jackie was so hot and thirsty, she considered getting off and asking Mrs. Torielli for a glass of water, but she didn't have time because Fiona told them to trot in the opposite direction. By giving Charlie a few good kicks with her outside leg, so Fiona wouldn't see how much trouble she was having, Jackie got Charlie started off at a decent speed and maintained it, although she had never worked so hard in her life.

"All right, ladies, that was fair. Prepare to canter," Fiona called and paused a moment. "And canter, please."

Eight horses began cantering around the ring. Some faster than others, some slower, but all cantering. Jackie kicked with her outside leg and pulled with her outside rein. Charlie didn't stir from his walk.

"Charlie," Jackie whispered to him. "What's the

matter? You ran for Dr. Mielzener, why can't you canter for me? Charlie, canter, please."

"What's going on there, Jackie? Canter."

Jackie kicked again, and it was like kicking the side of an oil drum.

"Please, Charlie," Jackie begged.

"Don't plead with your horse, Jackie. Make him canter. Aren't you carrying a stick? It looks as if you need one. Everyone walk."

Fiona climbed over the ring fence and went to a nearby tree where she ripped a branch from a limb; walking back, she skinned the little twigs off, but left a few leaves at the very end. Entering the ring, she handed the stick to Jackie. "I want you to use this behind the saddle, and hold on in case he gives a little buck. You have to maintain your discipline with him and make him do what you ask when you ask it."

"All right."

"Reverse, please," Fiona said, and everyone turned their horses toward the inside of the ring and went in the opposite direction. They walked for a while, and all the time Jackie tried to squeeze some alertness into Charlie because she knew they were going to canter soon.

"Canter, please."

Jackie was prepared this time with her legs, and when Charlie didn't canter right off, she hit him lightly on the rump. He swished his rear end underneath her.

"Hit him again, Jackie."

Jackie hit him again, but still not very hard. She didn't want to hit Charlie; she wanted him to canter because he wanted to do what she wanted. That seemed enough, and Charlie fell into a slow rolling canter.

It was a beautiful easy gait to sit to, and Jackie sat back comfortably to enjoy it. But at the first corner, Charlie broke into a trot, which jarred Jackie out of the saddle.

"Keep him cantering."

Jackie squeezed with her legs and tried to sit, but Charlie was trotting too fast and she was being thrown out of the saddle with every stride. Her knees were getting rubbed, and the stirrup leathers were cutting into her shins.

"Canter!" Fiona yelled.

Charlie had already trotted more than halfway around the ring, and her stomach was beginning to hurt. Then she lost her outside stirrup.

"Hit him!"

Jackie tried to reach around and hit him with her stick, but as she grabbed at both reins with one hand, she dropped them completely while at the same time hitting Charlie. He gave a little hop of annoyance with his rear end.

She was thrown forward, smashed her nose into his mane, then fell off to the left side, landing face forward in the dirt. Sitting up, she couldn't keep the tears out of her eyes. She had wanted everyone to be impressed with her new horse, and there she was falling off. And her nose hurt. Putting her fingers up, she felt it gingerly. It seemed to be the same shape it had been when she washed her face that morning.

"Are you all right?" Fiona asked coming over.

"I think so."

"Don't cry," Fiona said, pulling Jackie to her feet.

Fiona hated to see anyone cry. She didn't mind seeing them fall, but she wanted them to be made of rubber and bounce right back into the saddle without wasting time thinking about what had happened. "Then get back on." Fiona handed her the reins and walked away.

Jackie gathered up the reins and prepared to mount. "Come on, Charlie. Give me a break today, will you, please?" She mounted, settled herself, and had Charlie walk forward. But her knees seemed a little weak against the saddle, and she wasn't sure if Charlie kicked out again she would stay on any better than she had the first time.

Fiona didn't ask the class to canter again; everyone else had been cantering around and around while Jackie had been coping with Charlie. Instead, Fiona set up a few small jumps at various points about the ring. Only Katie and Lisa were jumping show-size fences because they had been riding the longest. The others had either just started riding or their horses weren't trained well enough to jump larger fences.

Jackie had known Fiona was going to set up low jumps, but they seemed very small from on top of Charlie. She knew that he was the best jumper in the class because he had already won so many ribbons. Even Ginger Ale hadn't done as much as Charlie had. Jumping ought to give her the perfect opportunity to show just how well schooled Charlie was, but it wouldn't be very impressive if they were trotting over two foot jumps.

Once Fiona saw how well Charlie could jump, Jackie was sure that they would be moved into the more advanced group with Lisa and Katie.

"All right, everyone. Let's trot first over the cavalletti, then go right over the small jump after it to warm the horses up. Line up behind Nan and do it."

Jackie found herself in the middle of the group with Linda right behind her. This was going to be simple. Moose had never been able to trot one stride for each pole lying on the ground. Instead, he had always managed to step on the poles, or hit them, scattering them apart so that Fiona would have to stop the class and set the poles back into place. No matter how short a distance there was between the poles, Moose never missed the chance to mess it all

up. Of course, Linda had the opposite problem. Diablo wouldn't trot at all, he would canter right through the cavalletti, and if she tried to slow him down, he would jump from one space to the next. No one could understand why Linda kept that horse. Or why she had even gotten him in the first place.

Lisa and Ginger Ale went through the cavalletti perfectly. Jackie, coming next in line, turned Charlie, making a good corner.

"This is going to be simple," she thought to herself rising into her hunt position. Charlie was trotting right out, and all she had to do was hold her reins steady.

Charlie trotted over the first rail and didn't hit it.

He trotted over the second, and Jackie felt him slowing down.

"Get after him, Jackie. Be there with your legs to encourage him to keep moving," Fiona said.

Jackie closed her legs on his sides, and Charlie slowed still further for the fourth rail.

"Kick him!"

They were practically going in slow motion, Charlie was trotting so lethargically. He made it over the fifth, and then he was supposed to jump.

It wasn't so much that he refused to jump. He was just at a standstill when he got there. Jackie sat, with Charlie in front of the fence looking around complacently.

"Jackie! Can't you do anything?" Linda yelled as Diablo came galloping down through the cavalletti, scattering the poles as he stepped on them. They rammed Charlie's rear end, jumped one end of the fence, hitting a standard as they went, knocking everything down and galloping across the length of the ring.

"What's going on here? This is organized chaos and it's supposed to be a riding lesson. You should have pulled Diablo up, Linda."

"And Jackie should have kept Charlie going." She spoke his name contemptuously.

"That's true, Jackie. You should have kept Charlie going. So let's start over and get Charlie to jump it this time."

Jackie turned Charlie, and while her back was turned to Fiona, she said loud enough for Charlie to hear "That's right, Charlie, you should have kept going. What do you want to be, a one horse traffic jam? Sometimes, Charles, you are just not very cooperative."

Chapter Six

On the way to Lisa's house a few days later, Jackie had plenty of time to relive the riding lesson. She had gone over it so many times already, she was getting tired of thinking about how badly it had gone; but she kept thinking about it anyway.

It was bad enough when things went wrong riding Moose, who wasn't expected to be super; but Charlie was supposed to be a trained show horse. She had told everyone that. He was supposed to canter, jump and behave. If Jackie didn't ask anything of him, he was fine. Walking was Charlie's idea of cooperation. But it had taken her all the rest of the lesson to make Charlie keep trotting and go over the fence. In the end it was still in slow motion, but he got over it.

And what had made Jackie the angriest of all, beyond Linda's making comments, beyond Nina's sitting on her super pony looking bored, beyond not being able to keep Charlie going, was the look on Charlie's face. When Jackie leaned down to look at him, she could have sworn there was a small smile on his lips. Smug. That's what he was.

Now that school was over, she would have more time to spend on him, which might help. She and Lisa were going on a trail ride today, after the blacksmith finished the three horses' feet. Maybe if Charlie saw Ginger gallop, he would want to keep up. If only Joanne were home, maybe she would know what was wrong with Charlie, but Joanne had gone to Colorado for the summer and wouldn't be back until the last part of August. So there was no help there.

Lisa said Charlie was probably homesick. Charlie had only had two other homes in his life, and he could feel strange being in a new place. Maybe he missed Joanne. Jackie didn't know if that was possible. All she knew was that Charlie was a beautiful looking horse, and he was the worst troublemaker around. Even Fiona had looked disgusted with him by the end of the lesson.

And the worst of it was that he had even become a problem at home. He had found one rail in the fence that he could slide out. Luckily, it was on the bottom, but she had to keep running out to make sure it was in place and put it back if it wasn't. She had found an old tire for him to play with, but he didn't want any part of that. Instead, he had found a big boulder in the pasture, one that was completely underground except for the very top twelve inches. He would stand with his two front feet up on the rock and stay there. Like a circus horse. He even did it in the stall where the foundation was exposed.

She didn't mind Charlie doing circus tricks like that if they kept him happy, but his second trick had nearly scared her to death. She had thought he was choking himself to death when she went out into his stall one morning and found him standing there with his mouth open and his tongue partially hanging out. Then, when she was on the verge of calling the vet, he stopped and seemed rather surprised to see her. The next time she caught him at it, she watched for a minute to see if there was something stuck in his mouth, but there wasn't. He just kept working his tongue around his mouth as if he had eaten a Bit O'Honey candy bar and it was stuck all over his teeth. There was nothing in his mouth, and he wasn't coughing or choking or doing anything except looking as if he were trying to spit his back teeth out.

Coming into Lisa's yard, she saw the farrier's yellow pickup truck with its small furnace smoking yellow coal smoke. Bud was one of the few farriers in the area who still hot-shoed, and when he agreed to take Charlie if Jackie would bring him down to the Griffins', Jackie was grateful.

In the 4-H club they had learned that hot shoeing was better; it was the older way and more time-consuming, but the horse got a better fitting shoe. The hoof wasn't cut to fit the size of the shoe, the shoe was contoured to the horse's hoof exactly. All the big show stables found someone who would make hot shoes, and Jackie felt lucky that Bud would take her on at all. He was very busy with the Hunt Club horses he did and all the other big stables. Bud didn't need Charlie, he turned private customers down all the time; Jackie knew that for a fact. He had turned down several of the club members because he was too busy.

So as Jackie slid off Charlie, she was proud that he was going to get the best set of shoes her money could provide.

Bud came out of the barn with a horseshoe in his hand. "Hi, Jackie. So that's Charlie. Well, stick him someplace. I'll be done with Moose in a minute."

Moose didn't have hot-shoes put on because he wasn't going to be asked to do anything very special anymore. His feet were big and round, and cold-shoes were good enough for him. But Ginger Ale always got hot-shoes, and now Charlie would have them.

Jackie brought Charlie down the aisle and put him in a stall. Now that the carpenters were gone, the electricity was on. She took off his tack and put on the halter that she had tied to the back of the saddle. Closing the door behind her, she watched Bud coming back into the barn. He was such a big man that he blocked almost all the light from the entrance as he stepped inside.

Bud wore blue jeans and a grayish leather apron to cover his legs. He wore a battered cowboy hat, which had a brown leather band. And she had never seen him without a wad of chewing tobacco in his mouth. If a horse was good about being shod, sometimes Bud would take tobacco out of the pack he kept in his back pocket and give some to the horse. He said they liked it. Like they liked beer.

Jackie hoped that Charlie wouldn't get any chewing tobacco for being good. She didn't want him picking up any expensive habits she would have to explain to her father.

Jackie came up and stood alongside Lisa, who was at Moose's head. If someone didn't stand at Moose's head, he would lean all his weight on the blacksmith, until Bud would stand up stiff. But if someone kept Moose's attention on other things, he was all right. It was a nuisance, but Moose was terrible about anyone working near his feet.

"I hope that Charlie horse has some manners," Bud

said with some difficulty because he had about six horseshoe nails sticking out of his mouth. He kept them there until he needed them so he wouldn't have to fumble in his box for them.

"Charlie is no trouble to work around. I can pick his feet without the slightest struggle."

"Charlie's problems start when she gets on him," Lisa said.

"Thanks, Lisa."

"It's true."

"No, it's not, he was . . ." Jackie started to say something about the vet but caught the look in Lisa's eye. She was right. Jackie didn't have to tell Bud about the vet; it would only give him a bad impression of Charlie. "I guess it's right."

"I don't care how bad he is when you get up on him, as long as he's no problem for me."

Jackie knew that, too. Every time Bud showed up, he'd tell them stories about the horses he had gone to shoe and they had given him so much trouble, he had told their owners they would either have to tranquilize the horse before he arrived or they would have to find someone else.

Jackie knew she'd never be able to give Charlie a shot of tranquilizer if he was bad. She could barely stick the needle into an orange without her hands shaking. Fiona had given her up as hopeless in that department long ago. So Jackie had brought a pocketful of carrots in case Charlie wasn't thrilled by the prospect of getting shod. Joanne said he didn't mind it at all, but Jackie was learning that that didn't mean much; lots of things Joanne had told her had little relationship to what Jackie was seeing. If she stood at his head and tempted him with carrots, maybe he would be good even if he had it in his mind to be contrary again.

"Okay, Lisa, Moose is done," Bud said standing up. He walked out to the doorway and spit some tobacco juice out onto the driveway. Jackie was used to that now and didn't even say yuck to herself. She went to the stall, brought Charlie back and snapped the cross-ties to his halter, one to each side. He was pointed away from the front entrance so Bud would be working with the hooves closest to the main light.

Bud came over and quickly pulled all four shoes off and studied the way Charlie stood. "He's not in bad shape. He's a little longer in the toe than I'd like to see, so I'll trim that down a bit more, help him break over faster."

Jackie knew that meant Charlie wouldn't be as prone to stumble and should have a smoother stride. "I wish you could make him go faster."

"A slow poke, huh?"

"Pretty slow."

Bud pulled a horseshoe from his back pocket and placed it on Charlie's hoof, moving it around and around until it settled in place and suited him. "He's a size one up front and aught behind. That's standard for his size."

"It's okay with me."

Bud then hooked the shoe back into his pocket and began trimming the hoof, then rasping it with a big file. It didn't hurt, any more than using a file on fingernails, unless the farrier went too far and quicked the horse. Jackie had given a talk on hooves to the club and had learned that inside the hoof was some blood at a level near the surface of the wall. That was the quick, and if a blacksmith took off too much hoof at once, he would hit the quick and draw blood. That did hurt the horse and might make him sore for a few days.

Bud worked on the other front hoof, then the back ones. He wanted the hooves trimmed completely before he began tacking shoes on, so he could determine if the horse was standing squarely when barefoot. Dropping the right rear hoof, Bud went back to his truck and Jackie could see him stoking up the small coal fire. Then he put the shoe in the furnace and held it in the hot coals for a while.

Jackie always waited to hear the music coming from the anvil when Bud began shaping the shoe. It was always the same. He tapped the shoe twice then tapped the anvil twice. Then back to the shoe, then the anvil. She had asked him once why he tapped

the anvil twice after every two times he tapped the shoe. He said he didn't know he did. She wished she were closer to the anvil because when the shoe came out of the fire, it would be red hot and then Bud would hit it with his mallet and little red pieces of metal would spark off. Hot shoeing was definitely better than cold shoeing; it was much more fun to watch.

Bud threw the shoe into a pail of water to cool it slightly then carried the shoe back into the barn, holding it in a long pair of tongs. He was going to put the shoe onto the hoof hot because he said it would make the hoof tacky and hold the shoe better.

At the first sizzle, Jackie could see Charlie stiffen, and his ears turned to the sound. Then the smoke started rising from the hoof, and Jackie could smell the burning hoof. Charlie sniffed a few times and rolled his eyes. She could see the whites around the brown. He stomped his hoof down on the concrete.

"Look out," Bud yelled as he ducked away.

Before Jackie could back away, Charlie had stepped back from her then spun completely around on the crossties without pulling either one out of the wall. Lisa grabbed Jackie by the arm and yanked her to the wall.

Charlie began backing up again, digging in with his feet to brace himself and broke both snaps. Realizing he was free, he made a dash for the front door, but Bud was standing in his way brandishing the tongs. Charlie slid and spun around again.

"Get the back door!" Bud yelled, and both Lisa and Jackie dashed for it, but Charlie was ahead of them in two strides. He didn't see the chain Lisa always put up across the doorway until he was almost upon it. When he did see it, he tried to stop, but he had too much speed going and started to slide.

He crouched down onto his rear end and slammed into one of the end stalls. He was shaking and snorting when Jackie got to him. Both knees were nicked up and his two hind fetlocks were bleeding slightly from where they had been scraped along the concrete.

"He's a feisty son of a gun, ain't he?" Bud called down the aisle.

She stroked his neck, and Charlie began to calm down. There would be no trail ride that day. She would be standing him in the pond to keep the swelling down.

"Charlie," she said holding his muzzle against the side of her face. "You aren't uncooperative. You're impossible."

Chapter
Seven

"WHY CAN'T WE HOLD OUR OWN SHOW?"

"The two of us?" Jackie asked Lisa as they cleaned tack on the lawn in front of the Griffin's barn.

"No, silly. The club. It takes about three weeks for the ribbons to be printed, so we could have it in a month. It would be preparation for the Fair. It's a good idea, isn't it?"

"You're crazy. Ribbons cost money. And besides," Jackie counted on her fingers, "four weeks from now is one week after the Fair. It's the week of the twelfth, or did you forget?"

"Twelfth? I thought twentieth. Oh boy. Anyway, we could have the show afterwards, and ribbons don't cost much when you buy in bulk."

"In bulk? Who's going to come to this show, everyone in the county?" Jackie asked dipping her sponge into the soap jar.

"I don't know. People would come."

"I think it might be better if we invited a few other clubs and kept it small. And didn't have printed ribbons."

"We'd have to have ribbons with our club name on them."

"You can tell Fiona all about it after the lesson, but she'll tell you to forget it if you're planning a big show. Our club is too new for that."

Lisa wiped her hand across her forehead and left a brown smudge. "How would we get people to come if we offered only a few classes."

"I don't know, but a full sixteen is too much for us."

"What if businesses donated the ribbons and trophies?"

Jackie looked at Lisa for a minute in disbelief. "That takes months to organize, not just four weeks."

"How do you know that?"

"I know."

It was a wonderful day to be lazy. It was warm, but there was enough breeze to keep the insects away, and there were big white clouds in the sky. It was a perfect day to have a lesson late in the afternoon so they could have all day to sit out in the sun.

Jackie looked out into the pasture and saw Charlie grazing alongside Moose and Ginger Ale. She was sure Moose didn't miss their rides; he was glad he could stand around and do nothing every day. Jackie couldn't tell what Charlie was thinking or what he was glad about. He was perfectly willing to go out on a trail, but once she got him into the ring, his whole attitude changed. In the woods or in the fields, with a little coaxing he would keep right up with Ginger; it was only in the ring he was so stubborn. She could canter him now, but it was more work for her to keep him going than it was for him to carry her around. And he jumped, but always so slowly no one thought he would clear the fence. Lessons had become a nightmare. Lisa said Charlie was still homesick but was getting over it. In a while, Charlie would come around, Lisa said. It was like breaking in a new car. Jackie wanted to know how long she had to wait for Charlie to make up his mind to go along with her.

"So you do think it's a good idea." Lisa said, pulling Jackie's thoughts back to the show.

"Sure. It's a wonderful idea," Jackie said, lying back on the grass and watching the clouds go by. "And we can have Bill Steinkraus judge the show."

"Really?" Lisa sat bolt upright.

"Don't be dumb. He wouldn't waste his time

judging a dinky little 4-H show where half the kids can't post on the correct diagonal. Fiona would have one of her friends judge, I guess."

"It would be great if we could have Steinkraus judge. An Olympic rider and all would bring a lot of people."

"Lisa! Where do you get these ideas?"

"Well, maybe if we couldn't get him, we could get some other famous person."

Lisa was going to start speculating, Jackie knew by the tone of her voice, so she just closed her eyes.

"Uh, Jackie . . ."

"What?"

"Jackie."

"What?"

"I think we're going to have a problem."

"Is it a secret?"

"The horses . . ."

"The horses what. Tell me!" Jackie sat up.

"The horses are loose!" Lisa shouted pointing out to the field.

Jackie jumped up. "So you sit there watching them do it? What took you so long to tell me?" She could see Moose bringing up the rear through a break in the far end of the fence. Charlie was out in front trotting down along the side of Griffin's property.

"Go get a bucket of grain!" Jackie shouted to Lisa.

"Go get a bucket of grain!" Lisa shouted to Jackie.

"Get the grain!" Jackie said and gave Lisa a little shove as she ran past her. "Get lead ropes! I'll try to keep them off the road!"

Jackie ran as fast as she could across the front field, but she knew it was useless to try to stop them at the road because Charlie was already there. "Charlie!" She screamed so he could hear her. "Stay off the road! Do you want to get hit?" He turned his head for a second to see her running toward him, then went into a canter so he could clear the stone wall at the end of the property. He made a fantastic jump over the wall, which Jackie had measured at three feet that spring. "You bum! You won't jump with me on you, but you'll jump by yourself!"

Ginger Ale and Moose scrambled over the wall after him.

She reached the road in time to see them disappearing over the crest in the road. If they kept going, she would never be able to keep up with them. The only way she could catch up would be if they stopped along the way. In her head, she went over the possible places that might lure a horse. A lush lawn would stop them, or other horses in a pasture by the road, or maybe some cows. On the other hand, dogs would keep them going, or a dump truck, or a bird in the tree. She knew it was useless to try to second-guess horses running loose—they were completely unpredictable—so she kept running down the road after them.

If they stopped at Mr. Waltham's, it would be all right because he liked animals and had always been nice to Lisa and Jackie when they had ridden past his house. He would understand.

If they stopped at Herron's farm, that would be all right because everyone there knew animals got loose and it wasn't anything people could help.

If they stopped at Mrs. Schiavo's, then it would be bad. Jackie and Lisa had learned to switch sides of the road when they approached her property because she didn't want dirty horses walking on her lawn making big prints all over. The last time the horses had come near her place, she had been pretty nasty about it.

As Jackie ran, she prayed that the horses would have sense enough to stay off Mrs. Schiavo's lawn. And prayed that Mr. Schiavo was at work. Everyone on the road knew he had a shotgun and wasn't afraid to use it. He had said it often enough for the whole state to know it.

Resting by the side of the road, she tried to stop breathing long enough to hear hoofbeats on the tar, but all she could hear was the blood pounding in her ears.

"Where are they?" Lisa asked running up to her,

three lead ropes wrapped around her neck and a bucket of grain banging against her leg.

"I don't know. Down there someplace." Jackie pointed.

"If they're in Mrs. Schiavo's yard, we've had it."

"I know. I know. Let's just keep going and hope Charlie would rather visit Herron's cows."

"Is Charlie leading this?" Lisa asked.

"Yes, the bum. What gets into him? What makes him be so bad?"

"A traumatic childhood? I don't know."

They kept running down the road, as Jackie took the bucket from Lisa, at the same time watching the sand at the roadside. "They've been this way. I can see tracks." Both girls were tiring, slowing down with each stride until neither thought they could keep going.

"There they are," Lisa said softly, and both stopped, then crouched behind a tree. The three horses were in a small abandoned pasture, not grazing, just looking.

"Okay, we can't let them see us and we have to keep them from going farther down the road. Let's see. I've got it. I'll stay up at this end with the grain and slowly walk in. You go to the other end and go in that way. We'll both go at once, that way we'll have both gates covered. Don't let them get past you. If you grab one, they'll all stop. Got it?"

"Got it."

"I'll signal you when you get there so we can surprise them at the same time."

Lisa nodded and began crawling down the road; if she stayed low the horses wouldn't be able to see her because of the stone wall and overgrown brush. When she reached the end, she looked back to Jackie, who waved her hand slightly and began walking into the pasture.

Charlie immediately turned his head toward her. "Come on, Charlie. I've got grain for you; you know how you love your grain. You wouldn't want to pass this up for something silly like a jaunt down the road, would you?" She kept talking to him as she slowly approached while shaking the bucket so the horses could hear the grain. "Charles," she said as sweetly as she could, "I want you to stand right where you are." Out of the corner of her eye, she saw Lisa coming in from the other end with a handful of grass extended to Moose. They would have them in a minute.

"Charlie, I want you to listen to reason and behave." She was almost close enough to touch his flank, and she took one hand off the bucket handle and reached out for his halter.

Charlie was off in one leap with the other two horses following. "Stop them, Lisa!"

Lisa stood in their path waving lead ropes in both

hands, but they skirted by her and ran back onto the road.

"Charlie! I could kill you!" Jackie screamed at him, running up to the road.

"I don't know what makes me think this, but I just know they're going to wind up in Mrs. Schiavo's yard," Lisa said, trying to untangle the ropes, which had wrapped around her legs.

"Don't say that," Jackie told her.

"Okay. I take it back. As if that'll make any difference."

They kept running, but they couldn't see the horses. As they passed each house, they scanned the front and back yards for a sign of the horses but couldn't see them, until they came up to the Schiavo's land and saw them in the neighboring yard.

"We've got them now!" Jackie said seeing that the only way out of the yard was the driveway because there was a three rail fence encircling the property. "I wish we had something to block the drive, a car or a gate. One of us is going to have to try to stand here, and the other is going to have to catch one of the horses. Do you think you can block the exit?"

"I was trying to block the whole field before, Jackie. I think I can cover the drive."

"All right. I was just asking. I'll go after Ginger."

"No, don't go for him. He sometimes kicks out when he gets loose. You'd better go for Charlie."

"Great." Jackie started walking through the yard hoping the people were out shopping and wouldn't see the commotion. Moose kept grazing on the lawn, but Charlie was already eyeing her from his position by the birdbath. "You're cornered now, Charlie, so give up before someone gets hurt, like you for instance." She held up the bucket and shook it, trying to tempt him over to her, then stopped. If she got too close, he might try to run again, so she held out some grain in her hand. "Please, Charlie. Please cooperate for once in your life."

Charlie was smiling again; she could see it as plain as the white markings on his face. He was smiling because he had the upper hand. Upper hoof. And she wished she could get close enough to punch him in the neck.

"Go on, Jackie, walk up to him," Lisa advised from behind.

"I'm afraid he'll run."

"Don't be dumb. There's a four-foot fence around this place, and I've got the drive blocked with garbage cans. We can't stand here all day; we'll miss our lesson."

"All right. All right. I don't know why I'm expected to work miracles. This horse doesn't want anyone near him. Come on, Charlie. Isn't it warm out here for you? Wouldn't you like to go back to a nice cool barn and rest for a few hours?" Jackie said

in her most coaxing voice, while she went on thinking that Charlie didn't need any rest. He was the most
rested looking horse she had ever seen. He looked
as if he could go on forever. And that was what was
scaring her.

As Jackie approached Charlie, she had to go alongside Ginger Ale, and the second Ginger caught sight
of her coming up from behind, he bolted across the
yard toward the big bay window. Jackie made a mad
dash across the ten feet that separated her from
Charlie, and she could feel the leather halter brush
against her hand as Charlie scooted away.

Jackie stood there and watched Charlie jump over the split rail fence into Mrs. Schiavo's yard, then ran to the fence and climbed over it as she saw Ginger Ale and Moose gallop down the road to catch Charlie. "You were supposed to stop them at the driveway!" she yelled to Lisa.

"Stop them? They nearly ran me down. What am I supposed to do, be smashed to bits?"

Charlie ran down into the Schiavo's back property, and Jackie closed her eyes as the other two horses followed him through what was obviously a vegetable garden.

"Aren't they ever going to stop?" Lisa wailed.

"You go this way, and I'll run around the front and try to head them off on the other side," Jackie told her, and ran as fast as she could around the house, hoping that Mrs. Schiavo wouldn't see her. As she reached the back yard, the three horses were paused at her end of the garden, and Jackie held her forefinger to her lips as a signal to Lisa. If they were quiet, perhaps they wouldn't be noticed.

There was the sudden sound of a window being thrown open; both Jackie and Lisa turned simultaneously toward the house. "Get those no-good horses out of my garden! You kids are nothing but trouble! I'm calling the police on you this time! I'm fed up with all these shenanigans in this neighborhood, and I'm holding you legally responsible for all damages to my garden!" Mrs. Schiavo screamed at the top of her lungs from the second floor, then slammed the window down.

All three horses jumped with a start and bolted back toward Lisa. Jackie followed Charlie, who had a stalk of corn sticking out of his mouth. She tried to estimate the loss, and from what she could see, there wasn't any. Somehow, the horses had managed to avoid all the plants, except Charlie's snack. But it was hard to tell. There were so many weeds, some were even taller than the corn. The squash vines were running rampant through the entire garden, and some were winding themselves up the cornstalks. The tomato plants weren't staked, and Jackie caught sight of a few rotten ones on the ground already. There weren't even any hoofprints in the ground because it was so tightly held together with weeds.

As Jackie rounded the house, she breathed a sigh of relief to see Lisa holding firmly onto Ginger, and the other horses standing quietly nearby. "How did you do it?" Jackie asked in amazement.

"I hid and when they went by, I jumped out and grabbed for anyone. I got Ginger," she explained, stroking her horse's nose.

"Thank goodness," Jackie said, clipping a lead rope onto Charlie.

The front screen door opened with a bang. "Get those horses out of the yard, you hoodlums! Get them out now, and I've already called the police!"

Jackie led Charlie onto the road, and Lisa led Moose and Ginger. When Jackie got past Mrs. Schiavo's property, she held the lead rope firmly in her hand and jerked it as hard as she could five times in quick succession. Charlie's head went up in surprise, and he stopped. She jerked him again with the rope, and he followed her.

"Don't you ever do this again, Charlie. Not ever, because this is the end of my patience. Next time you start running, you are on your own. Do I make myself clear?" she demanded to his face. "Be ashamed.

Have you no conscience at all?"

She knew he didn't because that smile was still on his lips.

"I don't see why Mrs. Schiavo's so upset. That garden was a mess before the horses ever got there, and they didn't ruin a thing."

"I can believe that. Every year it's the same story with them. They don't take care of the garden, and when nothing grows they blame it on the weather— too hot, too cold, too wet or too dry. Then there was the year they wanted to sue the seed company for selling bad seed. My father says he thinks they plant by throwing the seed out the back door and hope for the best. One year they accused Mr. Herron of spraying weed-killer when it was too windy and it drifted over and killed all their plants. My father said it was the tobacco fungus because Mr. Schiavo always has a stupid cigarette hanging out of his mouth and that can make plants sick."

"Is my father ever going to be angry if the police call him about this." Jackie moaned. "I can't even guess what'll happen this time."

"I think you'll find out soon enough," Lisa said.

"If there ever was a perfect time to take a horse and join a six-month cattle drive, this is it."

Chapter Eight

"Why is it every time you come home from the Griffins you have some horror story to tell us? I want some kind of explanation. This was supposed to be a safe, quiet horse who would stand trouble-free in the backyard until you wanted to ride him. First he drags the vet around the yard and sprains your ankle. Then he misbehaves in your lessons. Then he runs amok with the blacksmith. And now tonight, when I come home, I am greeted by the state police."

"They said he didn't do any damage to Mrs. Schiavo's garden."

"I'll thank you, young lady, to be quiet. I agreed to take this animal in because everyone assured me he would be a perfect gentleman and keep my daughter off the streets."

"We don't have streets, just road," she said softly.

"Jaqueline, please," her mother interjected.

"All that horse has done is keep her in the streets, running after him! He's got the whole town in an uproar."

"Now, Jim, I think you're the only one in an uproar," Mrs. Knapp said.

"Shouldn't I be? We are on the verge of a lawsuit. That monster could have ruined a whole vegetable garden single-handedly. What is he, some kind of radical bent on overthrowing the government? He could do it. He understands chaos perfectly. I'm serious. If that horse doesn't mend his ways, when Joanne gets back from Colorado, he is all hers again."

"Dad, that's not fair. Joanne will be going to college right after that and she doesn't want to be stuck with Charlie. And nothing he's done has been so bad. He got scared of the vet and all the noise in the yard. And the smoke from the hot shoes bothered him. You can't blame him for that."

"Don't stick up for him. Maybe he hasn't been so bad. Yet. And I'm sure Joanne doesn't want to be stuck with Charlie. That's why she stuck him with us. We wind up with a horse with a built-in wanderlust. No, Jackie, if you can't keep that horse in line, he's going. And if Joanne doesn't want him, someone else will I'm sure."

Even before Jackie could open her mouth to comment, she knew it would be a mistake. Once her father was convinced of something, it was hard to change his mind. And when he was convinced and angry at the same time, he couldn't be budged. She finished her dinner in silence, then went out to sit on Charlie's favorite rock.

He came over to her and blew his breath in her face, and she kissed his nose.

"Charlie, you are in a lot of trouble, if you don't know it." Charlie stood over her while she spoke. "Don't you like it here? You have a nice pasture and a comfortable barn. I know it's not fancy, but I'm trying to do the best I can for you. Can't you behave a little bit better? I don't mind falling off you, or having to work so hard to keep you moving in the ring, but if you could just knock off jumping out of your pasture and running down the road. People don't appreciate that. Don't get me wrong, I think it's a wonderful talent you have, but other people don't care for those tricks. Do you understand?"

Charlie sniffed at her again, then gave her a shove on the shoulder with his head.

"That's the kind of stuff you have to knock off. You're kidding around, but you kid too hard. I understand it, but my father definitely does not." She stood and put her arms around his neck, hugging the soft hair into her face. "Just give me a break, Charlie. I don't want you going to someone else. I want you here with me."

Charlie bent his neck and tried to grab onto the seat of her pants with his teeth. She pushed him away. "I wish I knew what to do with you," she told him and walked back to the house.

For the next week Jackie was very successful in keeping Charlie out of trouble. It rained a few days, then they had a lesson with the club, which was the best she had had so far. Charlie was still very slow, but she was able to keep him going enough to jump a simple course of fences, and Fiona said Jackie could show him in a few jumping classes at the Fair horse show. Fiona made Jackie carry a stick during the lessons, but Jackie didn't want to hit Charlie; she wanted him to be good because he wanted to please her. This aggravated Fiona, but Jackie knew that if she continued being nice to Charlie, he'd give in sooner or later, and she wouldn't have to hit him at all.

Jackie didn't expect to win any ribbons at the show. Lisa could do that. But if she could just finish the course with Charlie, if they could do what they were asked in the show ring even if they did it poorly, she was going to be happy. Of course, she didn't know how Charlie was going to react at a horse show. Joanne hadn't been exactly honest with them about Charlie so far. But if he didn't run away, go through the cow barn, bring down the rabbit tent and wind up in the middle of the art exhibit, Jackie decided she would be happy.

As Charlie walked along the road, Jackie didn't pay attention to where they were going. She could trust Charlie that far. He was safe on the road. Even when dump trucks passed, Charlie never even blinked. There was a good horse in him someplace, she knew it. He had all the talent he needed. He was fast; when he was running loose, he could easily keep way ahead of Ginger Ale. Just as long as no one was riding him. He could jump; he had jumped right into Mrs. Schiavo's yard over the four-foot fence, which Ginger and Moose wouldn't do. As long as no one was riding him. There was something twisted in his pea-sized brain, Jackie decided. He probably needed psychiatric rehabilitation.

"What took you so long?" Lisa asked, waiting at the prearranged meeting place.

"We dawdled," Jackie explained.

"Great. I've been waiting ten minutes already."

"Well, let's not keep talking about it. Let's get riding. Did you find out where the old quarry is?"

"Yes and no."

"Lisa."

"Wait. I called Mrs. Nyby, and from hunting she knows the country, but says it's been years since that trail has been used. It's badly overgrown, and she can't remember the exact spot."

"Good. No tourists."

"There wouldn't be anyway. It's up on the hillside and has been abandoned for about a hundred years. She said to follow the trail that goes towards Nina's, and there's a cutoff someplace by a big hickory tree. It's notched. If we follow that, there's a road, sort of, wide first then narrow. It will wind up the hill, real high. And if we're lucky, we'll find it."

"I'm game. Charlie is, too."

"That would be the day, Charlie going along with what you want. You're going to have to get firm with him and show him who's boss. I bet you'll have it out with him good, once, and you won't have to do it again."

"What makes you think so."

"All horses try to get away with murder. It's up to the owners to show them they can't."

"You never had a problem with Ginger," Jackie protested.

"Sure I did, but I didn't let it go. I laid down the law in the beginning. Once you let a horse get away with bad behavior, it eggs them on to try other things, and pretty soon you're stuck. And you're stuck right now."

Jackie thought about what Lisa was saying. Lisa did have more experience with horses and riding, and it was true she didn't have any trouble handling her horses.

"When you think about it," Lisa continued, "you're having the same problems with Charlie that you did with Moose."

"How do you figure that?"

"You can't make either of them work. One of these days you are going to get sick of Charlie's riding you; you're going to get really mad at him; then you'll be on the right track. But until then, you're going to suffer."

"Well, I like Charlie," Jackie protested.

"You don't have to defend him to me. I like him, too. I think he's a neat horse, but you're going to have to learn how to keep him from getting the better of you all the time."

"You'll see, Charlie will surprise us all, and soon."

"When he starts surprising us, let me know, will you? I wouldn't want to miss it."

"I won't have to tell you."

"Let's canter to the top of this field," Lisa suggested, putting Ginger Ale into a fast canter. Charlie followed without too much encouragement, but slower. It was up a hill; Jackie reasoned that was harder, especially since he was heavier than Ginger. It only figured he'd move slower. All of Charlie's food went to fat and none to energy.

They rode along the trail to Nina's, found the notched tree and made the turn. The trail was fairly clear for a while; they were able to ride in a straight line, but then the way became very overgrown. Only by seeing that there weren't any older trees in their way, just young saplings, could they tell they were still on the trail. And they had to work their way, constantly turning back and forth, to avoid trees and thick brush, in order to continue up the hillside until the trail opened up a little more and they could see where they were going.

When the trail widened again and became more of a road, they could ride side by side, but it was very steep, and they both had to stay in their hunt position for a long time. By doing that, the weight was taken off the horses, but both girls were feeling the strain on their legs and were relieved when the trail flattened out and they could sit down again.

Continuing along, they came upon a solid rock wall in the hillside. "This is it," Lisa announced as they stood in front of the rock.

Jackie stood in her stirrups, looking around the clearing in the woods. "This is it? This is all there is to a quarry?"

"What did you think it was?"

"I thought it was a big pit."

"I guess not," Lisa said scanning the area.

"Look, Lisa. There's another trail going further up the hill, maybe the pit's over there." Jackie kicked Charlie, and he trotted slowly through the quarry and as far along the trail as he could. Ducking branches again, Jackie reported, "I think there's a clearing up ahead."

"Be careful. Don't fall into the pit; I don't think I could explain that to your father."

Jackie came out of the woods onto a huge rock ledge that overlooked not only the quarry but several valleys as well. Lisa came out and halted beside her.

"Look, in that third valley," Jackie said. "That must be the Shepaug River." It looked like a piece of tinsel between the hills. "You can't even see any houses from here."

"I'll bet there must be a ten-mile view. It's too bad those pine trees block it."

"Not much. Can you imagine what it was like when this quarry was being worked? They must have used horses to pull the wagons, big draft horses, kind of like Moose."

"There weren't cars in those days or trucks, they had to do everything by hand. And they carved a whole hunk out of this mountain. Isn't it amazing?"

Walking carefully down the rocks, they went onto the quarry floor, where they noticed all the different colors in the rocks. Jackie dismounted and picked up several white pieces she wanted to bring home with her. She liked rocks, and whenever she saw an interesting one, she would take it with her.

When she remounted, she glanced at her watch. "We'd better get going. It's almost three, and it'll take me at least an hour to get home. I promised my mother I'd be home early today and be cleaned up by the time my father got there."

"Okay. We'll head back, but someday I'd like to have a picnic here."

"That's a good idea."

Charlie picked his way down the hillside, with Jackie crouched on his neck. They rode down the hill until they reached the spot where the trail should have widened. There they both stopped and searched. Jackie didn't think the area was familiar, but it was hard to tell because it was the middle of the woods and there were no landmarks to recognize.

"Are we lost?" Lisa asked.

Jackie paused for a moment. "If lost means we don't know where we are, then yes, we're lost."

"Boy, this is lousy luck."

"It's worse for me, I promised I'd be home."

"What about if we drop the reins and let the horses find their way home?"

"Get serious. That's only in the movies. If we keep going down, we're bound to come out someplace, so let's do that. We should hit the land the Hunt rides through."

"Sure," Lisa agreed, so they kept going, Charlie in the lead, moving carefully between the trees, not scraping Jackie's legs as Moose would have done.

Reaching the bottom of the hill, there was still no point of reference for them, and Jackie didn't know which way to go. If they went to the right, they might come out someplace on the other side of Katie's, wasting time. If they went to the left, they might get on one side of a barbed wire fence and there'd be no way to cross. Her sense of direction was usually pretty good, but with all the turning they had done to avoid trees and rocks, she didn't know quite which was the fastest way to go. She wasn't afraid; no one could really be lost on a horse in her town, but she did have to get home soon, and it was already three thirty.

"Left or right?" Jackie asked.

"Left," Lisa said. "I think it's toward my house."

"I think so too, if there's a way to get there," Jackie replied and headed toward the left, the direction she believed was out of the woods. They rode for a few minutes, the woods still thick, no clearings in sight.

"I hate riding like this, out in the middle of nowhere, branches snapping in my face. And in a hurry."

There was a small valley with a stream at the bottom facing the two girls. "I wonder if this is the stream that runs through Herron's farm?" Jackie thought out loud.

"I'll bet it is. That's the only big stream I know of."

"And if it is, all we have to do is go across it and up the hill and we'll be way up in back of your road. It won't be any trouble getting home from there."

"You go first. You know Ginger doesn't like to cross water in the lead."

"Okay." Jackie kicked Charlie, and he went down the slope to the water where he stopped and took a drink. "Enough, Charlie," Jackie said kicking him and trying to pull his head up. There was no response. She kicked again. Nothing. "This is no time to play around, I have to get home."

"Hey, Jackie. Look, over there across the stream. The trail looks like that bigger trail we were on. Maybe it's the other half of it. Looks pretty wide."

"Terrific. All we have to do is get there. Can't you try to get Ginger over the stream first?"

"I'll try." Lisa squeezed in beside Charlie and tried to maneuver her horse into the water, but Ginger just kept backing up and turning around. "He doesn't want to."

"Ginger doesn't want to! Charlie doesn't want to! I don't want to get off and wade through a stream because some horse doesn't want to get his feet wet!" She turned in the saddle and searched a nearby tree for a stick. Seeing a long, straight one, she grabbed it and pulled it off the tree so hard, the small tree bent

over. She held the stick in one hand, and the reins in the other.

"You're going forward when I tell you, Charlie, not when you're good and ready. Go forward!" She yelled, and cracked him on the rear end.

Charlie's head jerked up, and Jackie could feel his rear dip underneath her. In one leap, Charlie flew over the stream, and if Jackie hadn't grabbed his mane, she would have gone right off the back end. "Come on, Lisa," she called as Charlie galloped through the woods.

Jackie was really pleased. For once, Charlie was

galloping. And he was in front, too, no other horse was leading him; he was doing it all by himself. He was moving right along, and Jackie was having a terrific time watching the ground zip past under them.

"Jackie! Look out!" Lisa yelled.

Look out for what, Jackie thought, and raised her head. There was a thick branch hanging across the path. At first she thought if she crouched on his neck, they would get under it. Then she decided it was too low, and she should stop and go around it.

"Whoa, Charlie," she said, sitting back and pulling the reins. He didn't slow down. "Whoa. Walk. Stop!" Jackie pulled back with all her might, but because she had been so uncoordinated on the jump over the stream, her reins were too long and she struggled to shorten them. She tried sawing on the reins as hard as she could, but Charlie wasn't slowing down.

There was only one thing left to do. She kicked her feet free of the stirrups and jumped sideways out of the saddle.

"Are you all right?" Lisa asked.

Jackie could hear Charlie galloping away into the woods, snapping branches and thudding as he went. But of more immediate concern was the fact that her backside was wet. She turned her head and saw she had landed in a puddle.

"Oh, yoo-hoo," Lisa said. "Is anybody t'home?" And she started laughing. "Boy, did you look funny, trying to bail out," Lisa said between gales of laughter. "All these miles of reins in your hands, and Charlie running so fast we couldn't keep up. It was hysterical! I wish you could have seen it."

Jackie laughed, too, then stood up and shook the leaves from her. "I wish I had seen this puddle, so that I wouldn't be so dirty when I get home. The hysterics are going to be my mother's. Why couldn't he leave me off in a nice, dry spot instead of a mud hole?" They both started laughing again so hard that it was nearly impossible for them to both mount Ginger in order to track down Charlie.

"You say he was running fast?" Jackie asked, sitting behind Lisa, on Ginger's rump.

"Yes."

"See, Lisa, there's hope for him yet."

"Once you've got him moving, all you'll have to do is stay on."

"Right. No problem," Jackie answered.

"Right. And I've got this big can of glue at home, and we'll slop some on your saddle, and then you'll be all set."

Jackie could just picture that in her mind, and it started her laughing again.

Chapter
Nine

"OKAY, LADIES. WE'RE GETTING RIGHT DOWN TO THE deadline. One more lesson next week, and you'll be at the Fair just a few days later. Let's try to neaten our acts up today because next week, I want to go over braiding and showing in hand for those of you who haven't shown before."

Fiona was standing in the center of the ring with the club members positioned around her on their horses. Nearly all of the girls were very excited because showing was a treat for them.

Jackie wasn't sure if she was excited or not. She was still angry with Charlie for dumping her in the mud puddle during the trail ride. It wasn't so much that she was upset because she had fallen, as that she was mad because he had proved once again that he could run when he chose to and he never chose to do it at the right time. When her parents had seen her coming into the yard, mud from head to foot, there had been no way she could make excuses for him. As for showing, if Charlie was just going to drag himself through the classes, then she thought she might as well stay home. But she didn't really want to. The 4-H held the county fair only once each year and it was the culmination of a year's work for the members; to not ride was almost like denying that she had been a member of the club. Charlie wasn't going to spoil everything for her. Yet she knew that he could.

Maybe she should just call Joanne at the end of the month and tell her to take Charlie back. That was what her father wanted her to do. Maybe Charlie wasn't better than having no horse at all. If all he could ever be was impossible, then what good was he. Moose was better! But for now she still had Charlie and she was determined that today she wasn't going to make it easy for him. She had found a good stick to use, even before she had gotten in the ring. If he was going to make it difficult for her, she would make it difficult for him, too.

"Let's take the rail and walk. Not a slow walk, but a nice, brisk walk. The judge doesn't want to see you enter the ring and drag yourselves around."

Jackie tapped Charlie on the rear with the crop to

wake him up and make him walk faster. He moved along a little bit more freely than usual, but soon he was being passed by Diablo, who walked double time.

"Trot, please. And get your correct diagonal the first time and look down only with your eyes. I don't want to see your heads bending over for fifteen minutes trying to decide if you're right or not."

Jackie picked up the right diagonal and squeezed with her legs to get Charlie to trot. He never took the correct speed on his own; he always had to wait until she forced him into going faster. He would have jogged around the ring if she hadn't kept after him continuously. But her legs were getting used to the work after two months of tapping and squeezing.

They trotted and cantered for about twenty minutes. Fiona picked out various faults, trying to give them the impression of being in a class by having them halt and back as well as hand galloping. Then she had them walk, while she readied the fences for jumping.

That was Charlie's best and worst subject. He jumped well, but he was still slow. She never knew if he was really going to get over the jump or if he was going to slow up until he was just standing in front of the fence when he got there. If he did that to her at the show, she knew she would just die of embarrassment.

"Now, for you people entering the hunter classes,"

Fiona said, "I've heard by the grapevine there will probably be an in and out to jump. Some of you will have no trouble with that, but others will, so I want to get some practice on that first thing."

Jackie knew that meant Charlie and Diablo. They were the two worst horses in the class and could have trouble doing anything, no matter how simple it might be.

"Let's warm up over this first. Make a small circle to save time." They all lined up to trot over a jump made of a couple oil barrels lying on their side. After that Fiona had them canter around a set of low jumps, which no one had any problems with except Diablo, who went at his usual dead gallop.

Nina and Lisa jumped the more difficult course first, and neither of them had any trouble. Fiona wanted to save the troublemakers for last so she could keep them after the lesson without holding up the rest of the class.

Jackie walked Charlie around the ring, staying out of the way. She didn't pay attention to what the other riders were doing; she was just thinking how terrible it was going to be at the show when Charlie went around the courses in slow motion. She was going to be the laughingstock of the whole Fair.

"Are you ready to go, Jackie?" Fiona called to her, and Jackie came to the beginning of the course just as Linda was leaving the ring. "Your problem will be to maintain a snappy pace. If you are going to use your stick, use it before you enter the ring. Wake him up first, but if he slows during the course, will you please get after him?"

Jackie nodded. She'd do it, but she didn't want to be in the lesson. She didn't want to be on Charlie. She didn't want to have anything to do with him anymore. She started trotting her small circle, then put him into a canter and headed for the first fence.

It was a plain rail, and Charlie managed to haul himself over it, as he did the next three fences. The fifth was the in and out combination, two jumps set fairly close together to be jumped in rapid succession. Coming up to the in, Jackie felt him slowing down and squeezed him hard. He got over the first fence, and she felt him slowing as he neared the second. She kicked. He stopped.

"Jackie! You've got a stick. You could have used it. Take the in and out again and use the stick."

Jackie turned Charlie and brought him back to the end of the ring, then cantered toward the combination. Charlie started slowing again so she kicked him in front of the fence. He jumped the in and put on the brakes before he got to the out.

"Stick!" Fiona yelled.

Jackie brought her hand around and hit Charlie on the rear. He gave a little hop with his hind legs and stopped again.

"Jackie, please. Will you get after that horse? You've been torturing me for two months now. Why won't you hit him like you mean it? What are you afraid of?"

"I'm not afraid. I just don't want to hit him."

"Why not?"

Jackie didn't say anything; she just stared at Charlie's neck. Why didn't she? She had planned to, hadn't she? What was so hard about it?

"I can guess why. I go through it with everyone. You won't hit him because you love him. You don't want to hurt his feelings. Believe me, Jackie, you are doing him a disservice, because I've watched him take advantage of you all summer, and your patience has not paid off. All this horse will understand is firm punishment. If he stops in front of that fence again, I don't want you to turn him away as you've done a hundred times before. I want you to keep him in front of that fence and punish him for not doing what you want. I want you to take that stick and hit him as hard as you can about six times on his fat rear end. Tell him to go forward. And if you won't do it, you'd better forget about riding because you aren't going to be able to handle this horse, or any other horse for that matter."

Jackie raised her head and glared at Fiona.

"Well, are you going to do it or not?" Fiona demanded.

Jackie didn't want to do it. She didn't want to hit Charlie. She didn't think she even wanted to ride anymore. Yet somehow, she didn't want to admit defeat either.

"Answer me, Jackie, because we're wasting time. Yes or no," Fiona said impatiently.

"Yes," Jackie said through tight lips as she gave her rein a hard tug.

Charlie was ruining everything. She hadn't had any problems before he showed up and since she'd had him, nothing had gone right. He wasn't even as good as Moose, and Moose was nothing. Charlie was less than nothing.

And now she was going to have to try to get him over this in and out, and he wasn't going to do it. And Fiona wasn't going to lower the fences to make it easy.

She headed him for it, jumped the in and when she felt him slowing down for the out, brought her stick down as hard as she could on his rear end. Charlie took a leap off to the side, and Jackie flew out of the saddle, hitting the jump and bringing all the rails down with her.

Jackie didn't wait for Fiona to come to her, but got up, went back to Charlie and mounted. Bringing him around again, she jumped the in. He was maintaining good speed, and she prepared to jump. Just as he would have taken off, he stopped dead in front of it,

but Jackie kept going and cleared it beautifully, landing on the far side, on top of the ground rail. Coming back she remounted, holding the reins tightly in her hands to keep them from shaking.

"Charlie," she told him as they went back to the end of the ring. "I am so mad at you right now, if you know what's good for you, you will just jump that second fence even if you have to climb over it."

He jumped the in perfectly and kept his pace to the out, but something told her to brace herself in the saddle. She stayed on even though Charlie slid to a stop in front of the fence.

Jackie took her stick hand off the reins and began hitting Charlie on the rear as hard as she could. After the first blow, Charlie began to kick up with his back legs, but Jackie kept hitting him.

"Stick with him!" Fiona yelled to her.

Jackie hit him again, and he started to run around the ring, kicking first to one side then the other. It was all she could do to stay on, but she managed to keep hitting him. At the far end of the ring, she pulled him up and sat there for a second trying to catch her breath.

For once Charlie had been running when she wanted him to. She positioned Charlie for the in and out again. She was going to do it. She wasn't going to let Charlie ruin all her dreams. He had put her through too much.

He headed for the jump at a decent hunting pace and jumped the in in fine style. As he was going to take off for the out, Jackie brought the stick down on his rump, and he jumped that perfectly, too. Pulling him up at the end of the ring, she let the reins slip through her hands, then patted him on the neck. It had been as hard on him as it had been on her, for once. He was soaking wet.

"Thank you," Fiona said. "It's about time. Now you're getting someplace. Don't worry about him. You did the right thing. It was a favor to both of you, believe me. How does it feel to be able to handle your own horse?"

"It feels great. I just hope I won't have to do that in

front of every fence at the Fair."

"You won't, as long as you don't let him take advantage of you again."

Jackie nodded and walked Charlie out of the ring. For the first time in her life, she felt as if she had really been riding.

And from the way Charlie was puffing under her, she didn't think he had the energy to smile.

Chapter
Ten

Jackie let the back screen door slam as she walked out into the yard. The last thing she did every evening was to go out to the barn and pasture to make certain Charlie had enough water and that he hadn't gotten out. She glanced into the orchard but couldn't see him, so she assumed he was standing in his stall eating the hay she had left for him. There wasn't enough grass in the small pasture to support him without giving him hay as well.

Since the last riding lesson, she realized she needed more time with Charlie; she was just beginning to understand him. She had always thought that horses were to be ridden and had no minds of their own, but Charlie had shown her otherwise. He was a challenge, and she could conquer him if she could keep him. Riding, she now knew, was more than just jumping on and galloping across fields. It was Jackie thinking about what should happen, and doing what needed to be done to make sure it did happen. She knew there would be more problems as they went along, but she felt she would be able to handle them. And handle Charlie.

The perfect horse she had always wanted, she could see now would be the most boring horse in the world. It would be like riding a rocking horse. If every time she got up on a horse, it was the same, she would never grow as a rider.

Charlie was fun. Every time she rode, he was a little different. That's what gave him personality. And he had more personality than any horse in the club. If she had to give him back to Joanne, it would be like giving up before they could prove they were good enough to perform well together. The thing she had to do, now, was perform well in the show. That would make her father believe that she and Charlie had a new relationship.

It seemed to her that in every show she had ever attended, there was one horse who was the delinquent. Usually, it had been Diablo. It was possible that Charlie was going to be right up there with Diablo this time, but she was going to have faith in him and hope that they would do better.

Since the lesson, he had been very good with her. A few times he had slowed down, but when she carried a stick he would wake up. They had practiced jumps at Lisa's every day, and he hadn't refused, even over the bigger ones, the size they would jump at the Fair. If all he did was stop in front of a few fences in the show, no one would be interested in that because there were always horses who wouldn't jump for one reason or another.

Just as Jackie was reaching the shed, she heard her mother calling her from the house. "What?"

"Charlie's out."

"No," she said to herself. "Where is he?"

"He's down at Berlinghoff's."

Jackie ran into the barn for a lead rope. Since she had found that Charlie loved to escape, she always left a leather halter on him while he was outside. That made it a little easier to catch him.

Mrs. Knapp hurried out of the house and got into the car. "I'll drive you down."

"Okay," Jackie answered and slid into the car. "Was Mrs. Berlinghoff angry?"

"No. She thought it was kind of cute, Charlie standing under their apple trees, eating the windfalls."

"That's wonderful. He could get sick pigging down apples," Jackie said as they raced down the road.

"I never thought of that," her mother replied. "Maybe he didn't get too many."

"I hope not," Jackie said fervently. "I spend so much time picking up apples in his pasture so he won't eat them and colic, so what does he do but run away and get into someone else's apples. He's driving me crazy. I can't keep up with him. I have to be watching out for him every second or he's getting into trouble."

"He does seem to get into more than his share. Don't you think he might be too much for you, especially after you go back to school?"

"I'd cry for a hundred and twenty-five years if Charlie went away."

"That long! I guess you've gotten pretty attached to him."

"I love him. Don't you?"

"I suppose I'm beginning to like him a little. But I wouldn't cry for even a hundred and twenty-four years if he found another location to disrupt."

The car halted in Berlinghoff's drive, and Jackie jumped out and went into the side yard where Charlie was standing under an apple tree, but he wasn't eating.

"Charlie. Aren't you ashamed of yourself? Now stand there and we're going home. This is nonsense," Jackie said walking up to him, then quickly snapped the lead rope onto his halter. "You are a real disgrace, Charlie, now come on." She gave a tug on the rope and he followed her.

Mrs. Berlinghoff and her mother were talking in the driveway when Jackie went past. "I'm sorry Charlie got out. I hope he didn't do any damage."

"It's all right, Jackie. I was just startled when I looked up from doing the dishes and saw Charlie out there. At first, I thought he was a deer." Then she went back to speaking with Mrs. Knapp, and Jackie headed for home.

For once, Charlie seemed a bit embarrassed and followed her home with his head low, not making any attempt to snatch at grass along the way. Jackie turned him out in his pasture, but he just stood by the gate; she pushed him, but he didn't move.

"Charlie, don't tell me you made such a pig of yourself that you're sick."

He looked at her sadly, then brought his head around and tried to reach his stomach.

Jackie clipped the rope back on and tied his head lightly to the fence. "Charlie. This isn't the best time to get sick." She bent down and put her ear to his stomach. "Nothing. I can't hear anything."

Charlie began pawing the ground with a front hoof.

"Stop that. You'll tear up the grass. And hold still." She tried to listen again, but he was moving around too much.

Mrs. Knapp drove into the yard, and Jackie motioned for her to come over. "Hold Charlie's head. I have to listen to his stomach."

"Why?"

"Because if he's got colic, there will be no rumbling, and I think he's sick." She listened again and heard nothing. Untying the rope quickly, she began walking Charlie around the pasture. "Call the vet quick. Charlie has colic, and we have to get the vet up here."

"All right," Mrs. Knapp said and began walking to the house.

"Run, Mom! Charlie could die!"

Jackie kept him walking, then he pulled back on the rope and before she could stop him, he was down on the ground and rolling.

"Get up, Charlie, before you hurt yourself." She yanked, and he came to his feet. One of the former 4-H members had lost her horse when he had a bout of colic and rolled, twisting his gut and dying right in front of her. Jackie knew she had to keep Charlie up and walking.

"Jackie!" Mrs. Knapp called from the house, "I got the answering service. They're going to try to get Dr. Mielzener."

"They're going to TRY? Did you tell them this was an emergency?"

"Yes, but she wasn't very excited."

Mr. Knapp came around the side of the house. "What's going on out here, all this shouting? What's

Charlie doing now?"

"Charlie's got colic."

"So?"

"He could die. I told Mom to call the vet, but she can't get him; it's after hours."

"A vet bill."

"So what, Dad? Do you want Charlie to die?"

"No, of course not. If he needs the vet, he'll get the vet. Don't these guys work late on a Friday night?"

"I don't know."

"How did he get this colic thing?"

"By eating too many apples."

"I thought you were going to pick up all the apples so he wouldn't eat them."

"I do, Dad. He went down to Berlinghoff's."

"Out again. Jackie, we've got to do something about this horse. He's too much for one family to put up with."

"Jackie!" Mrs. Knapp called from the house. "Dr. Mielzener is on the phone and wants to talk to you."

"You've got to walk him, Dad," she said thrusting the rope into her father's hands. "Don't let him stop and don't let him get down on the ground and roll. That could kill him."

"Great."

She ran into the house and grabbed the phone. "Hello."

"Hi, Jackie. What's the problem with ol' Charlie?"

"I think he's got colic."

"What makes you think so?"

"He was eating apples down the road, and he looks uncomfortable. His eyebrows are worried and wrinkled, he keeps looking to his stomach and wants to paw the ground. When I started walking, he got down and rolled right over. I got him to his feet, and my father's out there walking him now."

"Did you take his pulse or his temperature?"

"No, I didn't have time."

"Okay. I guess your diagnosis is correct, but I can't get down there for a couple hours. You can handle it, though. But if it looks like you can't, I'll try to get there. All right?"

"I suppose."

"It's not too serious, really. Do you have any rye whiskey?"

"Rye whiskey?" Jackie asked.

"Yeah."

"Mom, do we have rye whiskey?"

Mrs. Knapp looked at her strangely. "Yes."

"Yes," Jackie reported back to Dr. Mielzener.

"Okay. Fill a Coke bottle half full of it and then fill the other half with warm water and pour it down his throat like a drench. Do you know what that is?"

"Is that when you put the horse's head up high so you force him to swallow?"

"That's right. Do that and keep him walking. If he

doesn't improve in about an hour, call again. Okay?"

"Okay. Is he in trouble?"

"I don't think so, if we watch him. Call me later to tell me how it's going."

"Bye," Jackie said and hung up the phone. "Where's this rye stuff?" Jackie asked her mother.

"What do you need it for?"

"For Charlie."

"That's strong liquor."

"Okay, so where is it?"

Mrs. Knapp went to a cabinet and looked. "I can't find it. I thought we had some left from when your uncle came up last Christmas." She kept looking while Jackie poured a bottle of Coke into a glass and rinsed the bottle out with water.

Mrs. Knapp stood up. "I remember now. When those two men from the Indiana plant came by a few months ago on that business trip, they finished off what was left. And it wasn't much, either. We don't have another bottle, Jackie."

"We need it. You'll have to go get some."

Mrs. Knapp looked to the clock on the wall. "It's almost eight. I don't think there'll be a liquor store open."

"Well, don't keep talking about it, maybe there's a place open in New Milford. It's Friday night. Things are open late."

"Right. I'll go." They both rushed out of the

house, and Jackie took the rope from her father.

"Now what?" he asked.

"We need some rye whiskey, and we don't have any. Mom's going for it."

"Hey, Sue, I'll go. You stay by the phone," he said and went to the car. Within a few seconds, he was off down the driveway.

"Don't worry, Jackie. I'm sure Charlie will be all right," Mrs. Knapp said, then went back into the house.

Jackie kept walking Charlie. It was getting darker out, and there was the occasional glint of green light from a lightning bug. Every time she slowed for an instant, Charlie was prepared to go down, so she had to walk fast.

"Charlie, please walk. This is important. You could die if you don't behave."

The thought of Charlie lying dead in his pasture was too much for her to consider. As recalcitrant as Charlie was, she didn't want to give him up, and she didn't want him to be in pain.

"Where's Dad, Charlie? It seems as if he's been gone for hours." She looked at her watch, but it was too dark to see the dial. New Milford was about ten miles away, and he should have been home sooner if he had been able to find a store open.

"Maybe we can go to each of the neighbors and they can donate a small amount into a pot until we have enough for you." She reached up and rubbed his forehead. "We'll get it somehow."

They walked and walked, then a car turned into the drive and it was her father. "I'll bring it out to you," he said and went into the house.

"See, everything's going to be all right, now," she said and walked Charlie out of the pasture toward the house so she could give him the drench by the porch-light.

Her parents came out, and Mr. Knapp held out the bottle to her. It was warm and smelled like the tavern down on Main Street in Danbury, where the door was open all summer.

"I can't reach high enough. I need a bucket," Jackie said.

"I'll hold Charlie," Mr. Knapp offered, and Mrs. Knapp brought the bucket she used for gardening.

Jackie stood on the bucket and struggled to get Charlie to raise his head then stuck the bottle into the side of his mouth and tried to pour. Nothing came out.

"What's going on? What are you doing, Charlie?" She looked and could see he was holding his tongue against the bottle, preventing the liquid from coming out. Jackie stuck her hand into his mouth, and he moved his tongue. She poured, and the liquid ran down her left arm, soaking her shirt; it splashed on her face, in her eyes, and wet her hair. When it was all

gone, she let Charlie have his head.

"I don't know if I got more on me than you got in you, Charles, but it's back to walking for us."

"You rest for a while, Jackie, I'll do it."

"No thanks, Dad. Charlie's my responsibility, and I'll do it."

"All right, but I'll stay out here with you. Stay by the back porch so you can see where you're going."

"He'll make dents in the lawn."

"It's all right this time."

She started walking him again.

"Do you know how silly I felt tonight?" Mr.

Knapp asked. "I thought that little package store down on Route Sixty-seven would be open, but it wasn't, so I had to drive down into New Milford proper. I never knew how much trouble it might be to live in a dry town."

"What's that mean?"

"It means you can't buy liquor here, and a restaurant can't serve it."

"Maybe that's why we don't have a restaurant."

"Maybe. So I found an open package store down by the railroad station. I parked and practically ran inside. The man behind the counter looked as if he expected I was going to hold him up, I was in such a hurry. Then he said 'Can I do something for you?' I said 'Yes. I need some rye whiskey for my horse.' And he didn't even blink. He just said, 'I guess you don't need our best whiskey, then.' Just like he had people coming in every day asking for liquor for their horses. I felt like a kook, I can tell you that," Mr. Knapp said, laughing.

"Thanks for going, Dad."

"It was no trouble, but I never expected I'd be doing that kind of thing when I said we could take this horse."

"I know he's a problem, but he doesn't mean to be. He can't help himself."

"That's not very reassuring. But we'll give him a while longer to see if we can't instill a sense of decency in him. And maybe a homing device. If he has to go away, maybe he can be trained to bring himself back."

"That would be nice," Jackie answered, and had to give the rope a tug. "Come on, Charlie."

For the past few minutes, he had been walking slower and slower, and Jackie's arm was stretched out straight behind her pulling him along. Now she was finding she had to lean most of her weight to keep him moving.

"What's wrong, Charlie?" she asked and stopped him by the light to look at him.

"Gee, Jackie, he looks kind of funny," Mr. Knapp observed.

He did look different to Jackie, too, and she became very frightened. His eyes were closing, and his ears were positioned like airplane wings instead of pointing toward the sky.

"Oh, Dad. It looks serious."

Charlie was swaying unsteadily on his feet, his head drooping lower and lower. His tail was swishing lazily back and forth; then he heaved a long sigh.

"I'd better call Dr. Mielzener and have him come right down."

"I don't know anything about horses, Jackie. But I'd bet anything our friend, Charles, is more than a little tipsy."

"Charlie's drunk?" Jackie asked.

"Call the vet and tell him, but I'll bet he is."

Mr. Knapp took the lead rope from Jackie, who raced for the kitchen door. She was just reaching for the phone when her father called from outside. "You can tell the vet Charlie just fertilized the lawn, too."

She smiled. Charlie was going to be all right.

Chapter
Eleven

EVERY TIME JACKIE RAISED UP THE SPONGE TO
Charlie's back to scrub him, water ran down her arm
and soaked her shirt. Her shorts were dripping wet,
and her sneakers oozed water. But at least Charlie was
standing there without putting up a fuss as Moose
would have. Lisa had started washing Ginger Ale before Jackie had arrived, and she was still at it; she
worked so slowly. Jackie knew Charlie would be in
his stall, braided and ready to go, before Ginger Ale
was. Jackie would wind up helping Lisa just to be
able to get out of the barn with a clear conscience.

For a while Jackie doubted if she would be able to
bring Charlie to the Fair, after his bout with colic.
But Dr. Mielzener had visted her Saturday morning,

and after checking Charlie over thoroughly said there was no reason to keep him home when the Fair was a week away. He told her to go lightly the first few times she rode, but by the last riding lesson, they would be all set, healthwise. If he had told her she couldn't attend the show, that would have been all right, too. What mattered was Charlie. Better than going to the show, she felt, was the fact that this week at the lesson, she had been included for the first time in the select group of Lisa and Nina. She had been allowed to jump the same courses and had done fairly well. Even Fiona had been impressed. Charlie did hop sort of sideways over the little coop and did get to slowing down when Jackie wasn't paying attention, but she felt as if they had really accomplished something together; no ribbon they could win in a show would be as good as knowing for herself that they had made progress.

Charlie stood still now while she hosed him down, except that he kept wanting to take a drink from the hose and wasn't happy until she put the nozzle in his mouth and held the control handle down. Water poured out the sides of his mouth, but she saw him swallowing. It would have been too easy for Charlie to drink out of a bucket like a normal horse. He had to do everything the hard way. Then with the sweat scraper, Jackie removed most of the water from his coat and led him into the barn to be braided.

Lisa was lucky to have a horse the color of Ginger Ale, with a dark brown mane; almost any color yarn could be used to braid, but Charlie's coat was so red that nothing would look right. There was no yarn made that could match that chestnut color. Jackie had decided to go with navy blue, the color of her riding jacket.

Taking a large comb out of her back pocket and a rubber band, she wet the comb in a bucket of water, stood on another overturned bucket and began combing Charlie's mane. When she measured the amount of hair for the first braid, she gathered the next hank of mane into the rubber band to keep it out of the way, then began braiding. She had told Lisa countless times that a good braid depends on the thumbs. Lisa never held the braid firmly enough with her thumbs, so the braid was always loose. Jackie held the hair tightly between her fingers and made good braids.

It took her longer than she had expected to do Charlie's mane because his neck was longer than Moose's, and she was trying to do the best job possible. Her first class would be Showing and Fitting, where the horses were shown in hand, and neatness counted heavily. When she got off the bucket, her fingers were cramped and her back was tired from standing in the same position for so long.

Jackie went around behind Charlie to begin combing out his tail. Lisa had just brought Ginger Ale into the barn and was preparing to start braiding, and Jackie wondered again if Lisa was slow on purpose.

Braiding the tail was worse than braiding the mane. The whole tail had to be done at once, not in separate parts like the mane, and horses didn't have it in them to keep their tails still for very long. The top part was always the hardest because there were a lot of short, fine hairs, and if the top wasn't tight, the job always looked sloppy.

First, she grasped a small strand from the left side and twisted it a few times, then she gathered some hair from the right side and brought both pieces together in the center. After twisting them together, she grasped more hair from the left side, then the right, braiding them together at the very center of his tailbone.

Jackie worked her way down until she was almost halfway done. Then she held the braid tightly in one hand and felt along Charlie's tailbone with the other hand to determine how much farther she had to go.

Charlie twitched his tail slightly.

"Don't, Charlie," Jackie said.

Charlie twitched it again.

"Charlie! Stop it!" she said firmly.

With two solid strokes, Charlie swung his tail left and right, going after a nonexistent fly, pulling hard enough to make her lose her grip on the braid. There was nothing she could do but let go. As soon as she did, Charlie relaxed and let his tail hang down again.

All the braids had loosened almost up to the top. There was no way she could go halfway back and start picking up again, so she pulled the comb out and went through all the work, straightening the tail to begin again.

"If you do that again," she told him, "you will be a horse in serious trouble." He flicked an ear back lazily to listen, then hung his head in an attempt to sleep. Jackie hoped he would stay like that for a while because all she needed was about ten minutes, and the job would be completed.

She got about halfway down again, and Charlie raised his head, rotating his ears from front to back, shifting his weight slightly from one side to the other.

"Don't, Charlie. I'm almost through, so be patient."

Charlie began to twitch his tail again.

Jackie straightened and grabbed the braid in her left hand. "STAND UP!" she bellowed.

Charlie jumped slightly at the tone of her voice, but didn't move an inch. He held his tail straight and firm, until Jackie reached the end of the tailbone and fastened off the braid with a small rubber band.

"Okay, kid, you can move now," she said.

"Gee, Jackie. You scared me, shouting like that. I was ready to stand at attention after that," Lisa commented from her bucket perch.

"It worked."

"Good. Are you finished?"

"No, I still have to bring the braid up into a loop and wrap the whole deal," Jackie said.

Lisa looked dismally at the rest of Ginger Ale's neck then at the few wispy braids she had already finished. "After you do that . . ."

"Yes, I'll help you finish Ginger Ale, but I want credit for it if the judge asks you if you did the braiding all by yourself."

"Oh sure, I'll say I had help."

Jackie walked back to Charlie. "I'll bet you will." She laughed and began to finish her own horse first.

Chapter
Twelve

GINGER ALE DECIDED HE DIDN'T WANT TO GO TO THE show. He didn't want any part of the horse trailer. He stood at the ramp with all his weight pulling against Lisa's lead rope so that he was nearly sitting down.

Jackie had heard it was bad luck for a horse not to load easily the day of a show, but she knew the only bad luck was that they were wasting time and giving Charlie ideas, too. She had his back turned away from the trailer and was allowing him to eat grass so he wouldn't pay attention to what Ginger Ale was doing. Horses were not very original in their behavior, and if Charlie saw Ginger Ale refuse to go into the trailer, he would think there was something wrong with the trailer and chances were that he would refuse as well.

"Lisa, why don't we see if Charlie will get in first," Jackie suggested. If Charlie got in, Ginger Ale might go in, too, and besides, Jackie would be of more help to Lisa than either one of the fathers, who really weren't too interested in getting dirty and didn't know the fine points of coaxing a horse in.

"Okay," Lisa agreed from inside the trailer. She began backing Ginger Ale down the ramp, then handed him over to her father. "What do you want, front or back?"

"I guess I'll take his head, you close the door behind him," Jackie told her, then walked Charlie in a circle to get a straight line toward the trailer.

Charlie walked along behind her and came up into the trailer. "Get the door," Jackie called, as she prepared to tie him, but Lisa wasn't ready, and in a flash, Charlie had backed out and was standing in the driveway looking at her.

Then Charlie wouldn't even get on the ramp. He did just what Ginger Ale had done. Stood there, and no amount of grain held out to him in a bucket could lure him inside. He just stretched his neck farther and father until he nearly lost his balance and fell on his face.

"We're going to be late. We're going to miss the Showing and Fitting class. I just know it," Lisa said

desperately. "We'll be lucky if we get there this afternoon at this rate."

In two minutes, Jackie knew Lisa would be crying; she felt frustrated that Lisa would waste energy on talking about what they weren't going to do instead of doing something.

She came down the ramp and threw the lead rope at Lisa. "You take his head, and don't let go no matter what he does. If he runs you to the bottom of the drive, you run with him, but don't let him get loose." Jackie walked past Lisa and went into the barn.

"Why do I get all the hard jobs? Why do you get

to stand around and I have to run after Charlie?" Lisa asked when Jackie came back.

"Because Charlie knows me, and he has the idea that if he doesn't behave, he'll get it from me." Jackie held up the broom. "Now walk him up the ramp and don't let him back out."

"I don't want you to hit him with the broom. What if he comes storming in and tramples me?"

"Just walk him in, Lisa," Jackie said, positioning herself by the side of the trailer. Charlie stopped again at the ramp and looked at Jackie out of the corner of his eye. "Get in, Charlie," Jackie said evenly and picked up the broom.

He started to shift his weight to his hind quarters, and Jackie grabbed the broom tighter. With a firm swing, she brought the bristles in contact with his rear end. In one stride, Charlie was in the trailer. Jackie dropped the broom and quickly closed the door behind him. Charlie was in.

Lisa tied him in the front and came out the side door. "That was easy. Now Ginger Ale will get right in." Lisa smiled and bounced off to get her horse.

Jackie shook her head and stood by the other stall, waiting to close the door on Ginger Ale. It didn't take much persuading to get Ginger in because he was fond of Charlie and wouldn't like to be left behind when Charlie was obviously going someplace.

After all the handles and locks were closed, Jackie double-checked to make sure they were secure, then headed for her parents' car. Lisa and her family got in their station wagon, and they all drove off.

Sitting in the front seat beside her father, Jackie felt nervous. She wasn't worried about riding; she was worried about how Charlie was traveling in the trailer. By the time they had reached the bottom of the drive, she could understand why Joanne had always bundled Charlie up before he went anyplace.

Jackie had spent over a half an hour wrapping his legs from his hooves to his knees with the heavy padding Joanne had left; then covered his hooves with white protective bell boots. And finally put a light cotton sheet on him. Joanne had told her to use it so he wouldn't rub his sides, and Jackie hadn't known what that meant. It seemed a little foolish to keep a sheet on a horse when it was already very warm, but she had left it on anyway.

From where Jackie was sitting, Charlie looked worse than the night he had colic. If he had walked the way he was trying to stand in the trailer, he would have been staggering. First he was tipping to the left, then to the right. When the car made a slight corner, Charlie landed with so much force on the wall, the whole trailer shook.

"What's Charlie doing?" her father asked.

"I don't know," Jackie answered, her eyes glued on

the chestnut rear end. "It looks as if he's trying to balance on two feet. He's going to kill himself."

"Nonsense. He'll be fine."

"He won't be fine," Jackie retorted; then as Charlie lurched sideways, she gasped. "There he goes again. I wish Mr. Griffin would slow down. He's not flying a jet now."

"He's only going twenty-five miles an hour. Charlie will be all right. It's not much farther, just a few miles."

Jackie was on the edge of her seat watching Charlie. He had even stirred Ginger Ale up; every time Charlie banged against the partition, the dun horse tried to jump out of the way. The corners were the worst; Charlie would dip down so low that his back was nearly invisible, and with the car window open, Jackie could hear him scrambling, trying to keep his balance. She could only hope the bandages would stay up through all this activity, because if they didn't, Charlie was going to be injured. He ran the risk of being hurt even with the wrappings on; only armor could have protected him.

The show grounds were just up ahead; Jackie could see the tents and trailers already there; and she breathed a sigh of relief. Charlie had made it safely. All they had to do was turn off the main road, go down the side road and then pull onto the show grounds. Charlie just had to hang on about five minutes more, and he would be on firm ground.

Mr. Griffin braked the trailer and turned the corner carefully off the main road. At that moment, Charlie had been shifting his weight again and disappeared.

"Beep the horn, Dad! Charlie's gone down!"

"What?"

"Honk the horn! Charlie's down! Stop the car!" Jackie shouted.

Mr. Knapp stopped the car, but Jackie was already out and running down the road to the trailer. Lisa met her there and both girls jumped up onto the hinges and looked over the ramp into the stalls. Charlie was sitting with his legs underneath him, looking like a duck nesting on the floor of the trailer. He turned his head to see Jackie and didn't seem to be the least bit upset.

"How are we going to get him out?" Lisa cried. "What if his legs tangle, get caught under the partition or something?"

"Just go to his head and stand there. I'll get the ramp."

Lisa ran around to the side door. "Do I unclip the lead rope?"

"Of course," Jackie said and heard the door open. She quickly undid all the latches and handles to the ramp and door and opened the back of the trailer while Charlie watched her the entire time. "Okay,

Charlie, get up," Jackie said and patted him. "Lift his head a little, Lisa."

But Lisa didn't have to do anything. Charlie stood up and backed down the ramp. Jackie grabbed the lead rope as he went by her, and he looked around as if nothing had happened.

"I'd better lead him over," Jackie said as Charlie began trotting her down the center of the road. She pushed him onto the grass and gave the lead shank a tug to bring him to a walk. Looking his legs over as best she could, she saw that the back wrappings had held up better than those in front. There was a tear in the right inside one, and she could see a spot of red on the white material. Charlie was bleeding, and she hoped it wasn't serious. It would be terrible if he had to have stitches taken. There would be a scar for sure, and he didn't have any blemishes. It would be worse if he had broken any of those tiny bones in his hooves. He might never recover.

"From the way you're acting right now, Charlie, you don't seem to be hurt too badly," she told him and patted his neck. He was still surveying the scene with great interest and wasn't favoring any of his legs. The wrappings would have to come off before Jackie could determine how much damage he had done to himself.

The Griffins passed her in their car, and her parents followed, parking under a group of trees not far from the English ring. Jackie arrived and handed the lead shank to her father so he could hold Charlie while she removed the leg wraps. When Lisa had brought Ginger Ale out and tied him to the trailer, Jackie asked her to find Fiona, who would know how seriously Charlie was injured.

Both hind legs seemed to be in good shape, but the right front had several scrapes and was bleeding from a cut on the inside of the cannon bone. On the left leg, there was a large scrape on the fetlock, which was bleeding. His cotton sheet was soaked and his neck was foamy with salty perspiration, but otherwise, Charlie seemed happy enough.

Jackie removed the sheet, tried wiping off the sweat, but she knew if she was going to be able to get him in the show ring at all, he should be rinsed off. Even if she didn't show, he would feel very sticky with all that sweat on him. His braids were still intact, and his tail was still wrapped tightly. He hadn't managed to mangle that.

Fiona came running over with Lisa and crouched beside Charlie's legs, feeling the bones with her fingers. "He must have had a terrible ride," she remarked, running her hand down the front of his cannon bone, then the back. "It seems to be all right. This is just surface blood," she told Jackie, pointing to the cut on his fetlock. "The vet wouldn't even stitch this one," she said about the one on his right leg. "If he's not sore, ride him. If he starts getting ouchy during the day, scratch the classes, but I think he'll be all right. If that's all that happened, you were both lucky. Horses have killed themselves in trailers doing just about the same thing."

"I think I should rinse him off before the Showing and Fitting class."

"That would be a good idea, and tell the judge that Charlie got a little banged up in the trailer. That will be enough to explain why you have ointment on his legs. You do have some Furacin or something with you, right?"

"It's in my tack box," Lisa answered.

"That's good. Wash him off, put the ointment on, and go into the class. You really were lucky, Jackie," Fiona said as she turned around to leave.

"I guess so," Jackie replied and turned toward Charlie. He turned his head quickly toward her and smashed into her face hard enough to make her eyes water.

"Charlie, can't you ever be careful? Why do you always have to be so impossible?" She handed the rope back to her father, picked up a bucket and began walking toward the spigot where she could get water. Maybe it was bad luck after all when a horse didn't get right in the trailer.

Chapter
Thirteen

IT SEEMED VERY HOT FOR JACKIE, STANDING IN THE middle of the ring while the judge inspected each horse in the Showing and Fitting class. All Charlie wanted to do was either put his head down and eat all the grass that was growing in the center of the ring or go over and visit the horses standing next to him. Jackie knew if she didn't pay strict attention to him, he'd start walking away from her. She couldn't blame him, the class seemed to be going on forever. Some judges could make their decisions fast and others couldn't make up their minds at all.

Charlie sneezed and got his white nose dirty; Jackie produced a tissue from her jacket pocket and wiped it clean. She knew he was getting bored and just hoped he would keep his patience long enough for the class to be dismissed.

Finally the judge approached them, standing back to get an overall view of Charlie; then she wiped her hand down Charlie's back and looked at it. Jackie knew he was clean; she had scrubbed him until his skin was practically pink.

"What happened to his leg?" the judge asked, picking up Charlie's left hoof to determine if Jackie had cleaned it before entering the ring.

"He got a little banged up in the trailer, but it just seems to be surface abrasions. I washed his legs, dried them and put Furacin ointment on them."

The judge nodded slightly. "Does he have fly spray on him?"

"No," Jackie answered. Fly spray could make the coat sticky, and she didn't think there would be many flies out first thing in the morning, so she put off applying it until later in the afternoon.

"Did you do the braiding yourself?"

"Yes, I did."

The judge nodded again, walking around Charlie slowly, and Charlie kept leaning on the reins trying to get to her. Jackie knew Charlie just wanted a chance to sneeze on her jacket, but she managed to keep his head away from the judge.

Jackie thought they might have a chance at a ribbon in that class because Charlie did look neat. Some of the other horses had very long manes that were braided into big loops, and that wasn't proper. A few horses had bows in their manes, and there were little green pompoms on a palomino horse. Those weren't right at all. One appaloosa horse had stains on his cream-colored hocks, and while Jackie could sympathize with that, she knew that would take points off the girl's score.

Charlie's white socks were perfectly clean, and there was no dandruff in his coat. His tail was immaculate, even underneath the tailbone, and the braids were good. It depended on the judge's taste and how much she might take off for the scrapes on his legs.

The judge stood to the side of the ring and looked them all over once again, checking their numbers, then walked to the announcer's booth and handed in her score card. The ribbons and a small silver plate were handed to the ring steward, and she walked to the center of the line of contestants.

"Ladies and gentlemen," the announcer called over the loudspeaker. "We have the results of Class Number One in the English ring, Junior Showing and Fitting. First-place ribbon and trophy is awarded to number fifty-seven, Nina Torielli and Butterfly. Second place goes to number thirty-one, Jackie Knapp and Impossible Charlie. Third place goes to . . ."

Jackie stepped forward in amazement to receive her red ribbon, which was hooked onto the browband of Charlie's bridle; she kissed his muzzle and trotted him from the ring while the ribbon fluttered in the breeze.

Her parents were waiting and hugged her as soon as she left the ring. Her mother even hugged Charlie, and her father patted him soundly on the neck.

"Since when has his name been Impossible Charlie?" her mother questioned as they reached the trailer.

Jackie shrugged. "Since I sent in the entry blank. I didn't know what else his name could be, and it was just something that came to my mind. I didn't figure I could just call him Plain Charlie. I didn't want to call him Charlie Brown."

"I don't care what you call him, it's wonderful that you got second place. Lisa got a fifth, did you hear that?" Mrs. Knapp said.

"She did? Good. It must have been the braids; they were a little loose this morning. Lisa did half the neck and I did the other half." Jackie took the saddle from the trunk of the car, then hoisted it up onto Charlie's back, smoothing the saddle pad as she did.

"That's great, Jackie," Lisa said, coming up to the trailer. "Your first red ribbon. You really should have gotten the blue. Nina was no better with Butterfly than Charlie was."

"I'm glad we got the second, considering what

Charlie went through to get here. Hurry up and get tacked, or you'll miss our next class." Jackie mounted and got herself straightened in the saddle, making sure her jacket was not underneath her and the collar was lying flat.

"Go out to the warmup area, and I'll meet you there in a minute."

"Okay," Jackie answered and steered Charlie away from the trailer and crowds.

There were a few people in the warmup field. Several western riders were loping slowly along, the brightly colored fringe on their chaps flapping as they went. Charlie walked without being upset by anything going on. He was fascinated by the sheep who passed and the sounds they made; he tried to look into each tent, especially the ones with the poultry because they were making strange noises, too.

She reached down and patted his neck, feeling very happy. It was nice winning the second place in the Showing and Fitting, but it was nicer still to have her own horse. She might have to struggle with him; but that was just the way he was.

The class was called and Jackie returned to the English ring just as Lisa was scrambling aboard Ginger Ale. The steward opened the in-gate, and everyone entered. Finding herself in an open space, Jackie positioned herself next to the rail. If she stayed there, she had a better chance of avoiding other horses. Riders tended to go toward the inside of the ring, leaving space on the rail. A good judge could see the riders on the inside as well as those near the rail, so it was better to be there.

The contestants walked until the judge had written everyone's number on her scorecard, then the ringmaster asked them to trot. Everyone began trotting, and soon Jackie was being passed on the inside by faster horses.

She got Charlie into a decent trot for him and tried to maintain that steady pace, even if it was a bit slow. She tried to remember everything about her equitation. Heels down, hands down, head up, back straight. And relax.

They were told to walk, which Charlie did readily, and Jackie gathered her reins, preparing to canter.

"Canter, please," came the call, and Jackie was ready. For once Charlie started right off and on the correct lead, too. He went at a slow, steady pace, and she sat back, relaxing more than she had at the trot. If Charlie kept going like that, everything would be fine.

Jackie heard some hoofbeats coming up behind her and glanced sideways to see a skinny cream-colored horse beside her; but instead of passing, the girl just stayed there. That was all right; Charlie wouldn't do anything, but the girl was blocking Jackie from the judge's view, so Jackie decided she would try to move away as soon as she had the space.

"Outside!"

Jackie could tell by the voice who was coming up behind her. Linda and Diablo, who was probably running away again. There wasn't any room for Linda to squeeze in beside her, but Linda tried anyway, pushing into Charlie and causing him to break into a trot. Jackie looked up and saw the judge looking right at them. She got Charlie back into a canter just as the ringmaster was calling for a walk again.

The rest of the class went off without incident, but Jackie knew, when they were lined up for the ribbons to be pinned, they didn't have any hope of winning anything. Thanks to Linda. Lisa picked up a third, and after the other places were called, the class was dismissed.

Jackie stroked Charlie's neck. "It wasn't your fault. I wouldn't have blamed you if you had kicked Diablo; he sure deserved it."

Dismounting, then loosening the girth, Jackie bent down and ran her hand along Charlie's legs. If there was any swelling, she was going to scratch the remainder of the classes. Showing wasn't important if Charlie was uncomfortable. But he seemed all right. Back at the trailer, she wiped the sweat from his face and was preparing to remove the saddle since she was not scheduled to ride in another class for over an hour.

"May I have your attention please," the announcer called. "There has been a change in the schedule in the English ring. Classes Twelve, Thirteen, Fourteen, and Fifteen will be held after Class Number Three." The announcer repeated the message; Lisa and Jackie looked at each other in bewilderment.

"I don't get it. They usually run all the flat classes in the morning and all the jumping in the afternoon," Lisa remarked. "They hate to put up the jumps twice in the same show."

Jackie shrugged. "Don't ask me. Maybe they think it's better to jump when it's cool."

"I'd rather hack when it's cool. Not that it will ever be cool today. A jumping class goes on forever, but each horse is only ridden for a minute. I hate going around and around at four in the afternoon when the ring is all dusty and the horses are dead tired. Remember the time Patti Stankowski almost fainted in a pleasure horse class?"

"Yeah. I thought her mother was going to murder the judge." Jackie tightened the girth again because she was riding in Class Thirteen, hunter over fences. The ponies were to go first in Class Twelve, but Jackie could see there weren't many of them lining up by the in-gate, and it would be her turn to go very shortly. She waited until all the ponies had jumped before she mounted Charlie and began walking to limber him.

Having checked the course earlier that morning, she went over it again in her mind.

Lisa came up and stood beside Jackie in line while Nina won the pony hunter class. It didn't surprise them; Nina's pony was adorable, just like a miniature thoroughbred.

"Don't you wish Charlie would behave like Nina's pony?" Lisa asked.

"I like Charlie just as he is. He's fun because he has a mind of his own. But if he's going to be bad, he'd better prepare himself to fight it out with me from now on," Jackie said with determination.

"That's all it takes."

"I know that—now. Let's just hope it doesn't take Charlie as long to get the message as it did for me."

"Horses learn fast who's boss. It takes people longer."

The ringmaster opened the in-gate for the first horse, and everyone stood there looking at each other, no one wanting to be the first horse into the ring. Jackie nodded in assent. "I'll go," she offered.

"No, don't be stupid," Lisa whispered. "Let someone else go first so you can see the course."

"I'll go," Jackie said again, steering Charlie through the crowd. She didn't care if she went first or not, but it was silly for all of them to sit there waiting for someone to go when no one wanted to go first.

"Number Thirty-one," the ringmaster called to

the judge, and Jackie began trotting her circle. She started Charlie into a canter early in case he didn't take it easily, but he did and she got him going in a fair hunter pace, then rose into her half-seat jumping position.

It was a simple figure-eight course with four fences on the rail and one in the middle. That would be the hardest, Jackie knew, because the horses would have to change their lead in the center and some might not care for that. She wasn't sure if Charlie could do it, but she decided she would just trust him.

As they approached the first fence, she tapped him lightly on the shoulder just to remind him that she was carrying a crop, and he picked up a little speed. They jumped it smoothly and went straight onto the second fence, which presented no problems. They rounded the top of the ring and headed for the third.

Jackie became a bit concerned. They had to make a sharp corner after the fence and she wasn't sure how to do it. Charlie jumped the fence in the middle, and Jackie had to pull him quickly off the track or he would have kept going and jumped the sixth fence from the wrong direction.

Going through the middle was choppy; Charlie was shifting his weight, trying to find out where they were going. He jumped the middle fence, landing on the wrong lead, but after the fifth fence, she leaned enough to the inside, and he picked up his correct lead. They completed the rest of the course, and she trotted out of the ring.

Fiona was waiting for her at the out-gate. "Nice job, Jackie. Not too smooth through the middle but all right. If you had kept him to the rail, you would have had more room to go from the third fence through the middle. I guess we can start working on that now, seeing as how you've learned to keep him going." Fiona smiled and went back to the rail to see how the other riders were doing.

Jackie slid off, loosened the girth and ran up her stirrups, then rubbed the sweaty spot behind Charlie's ear. He always enjoyed that.

"Thank you for being so good. I'm just glad we got around the whole course without crashing, Chuck," she whispered into his ear, and he rubbed his head against her with such force that she had to struggle to keep her balance. She just laughed. He was never going to stop being Charlie.

Her parents came over and congratulated her on the good job she and Charlie had done. Jackie didn't care that they weren't going to win a ribbon; they had done well for them, and she knew her father wasn't going to take Charlie away now that she could handle him pretty well. Though Charlie wasn't exactly like the horse of her dreams, he was better because he was a real horse.

The class finished, and the jumps were being low-

ered for the next pony class as Jackie walked Charlie to cool him. She had seen Lisa's trip and it had been a good one, but then Lisa and Ginger Ale were a good team and had won many classes because of that. Someday she and Charlie would be a good team.

"Would the following horses please enter the English ring," the announcer called. "Numbers forty-five, ninety-eight, ninety-three, fourteen, twenty-seven, one hundred and six, thirty-one and one hundred and fifty-two. Will those horses please enter the English ring."

Lisa turned Ginger around and began trotting for

the ring. "Come on, Jackie. You got a call back!"

Jackie turned Charlie and began trotting after Lisa, whose number had been called second, not believing she had heard correctly. As she entered the ring, she went up to the ringmaster. "Did they call number thirty-one?"

"Yes," the man answered.

Jackie shook her head and lined up facing the announcer's booth. Getting called for a reserve was practically as good as being pinned. No ribbons were given, but it was a commendation of sorts and Jackie was delighted.

"Ladies and gentlemen, we have the results of Class Number Thirteen, hunter over fences. Blue ribbon and trophy goes to number foutreen, Jumpin' Jack owned by Rita Gagliardi. Second place goes to Sonatina owned by Dale Sharp."

Jackie looked across the ring to Lisa with surprise. They were calling the places in a different order from the numbers as they had been given.

"Third place ribbon goes to number ninety-eight, Ginger Ale, owned by Lisa Griffin."

Jackie applauded as Lisa walked forward to receive her yellow ribbon.

"Fourth place goes to number thirty-one, Impossible Charlie, owned by Jackie Knapp."

Jackie couldn't believe what she was hearing. She threw her arms around Charlie's head and kissed him as hard as she could. Then, laughing, she walked forward to receive her white ribbon, which was hung on Charlie's bridle. As they went toward the out-gate, the judge approached smiling.

"He's a very cute horse, and I really liked him. If you had been smoother in your transition at the middle fence, you might have placed even higher. You should try for a bit more speed, too."

"Thank you," Jackie managed to say and left the ring.

Everyone was hugging her and Charlie, patting them and cheering. Getting a fourth for Charlie was a real accomplishment. As the crowd thinned out and she was able to make her way back to the trailer, she just kept looking Charlie in the face and shaking her head in disbelief.

She slid the bridle off and replaced it with a halter so he could have a drink and a few bites of hay before the next class. Then she held her arms around his head and kissed the soft skin by his eye. "I guess you're sort of possible after all," she told him.

He shoved his head against her so hard that she lost her balance and fell against his water bucket, splashing water all over her jodhpurs and soaking her boots.

And Charlie was smiling.

Again.